The Shakespeare Folio

The Shakespeare Folio

Chris Eyles

INSOMNIAC PRESS

Library and Archives Canada Cataloguing in Publication

Eyles, Chris, 1988-, author
The Shakespeare folio / Chris Eyles.

Issued in print and electronic formats.
ISBN 978-1-55483-189-0 (softcover)
ISBN 978-1-55483-203-3 (HTML)

I. Title.

PS8609.Y54S53 2017   C813'.6   C2017-903989-X
                            C2017-903990-3

The publisher gratefully acknowledges the support of the
Canada Council for the Arts and the Ontario Arts Council.

Printed and bound in Canada

Insomniac Press
520 Princess Avenue, London, Ontario, Canada, N6B 2B8
www.insomniacpress.com

THE CANADA COUNCIL | LE CONSEIL DES ARTS
FOR THE ARTS | DU CANADA
SINCE 1957 | DEPUIS 1957

ONTARIO ARTS COUNCIL
CONSEIL DES ARTS DE L'ONTARIO

For my friends and family who have supported me since the beginning. And thanks to the people, movies, shows, and games that inspire my creativity. I hope you enjoy reading this as much as I did writing it.

I would like to thank the librarians at the Thomas Fisher Rare Book Library for allowing me access to my inspiration for this book, the actual Shakespeare Folio. The wonderful team at Insomniac Press for their efforts putting this work into print. Those family and friends whom I made read early drafts to give feedback as well as bounced ideas off of. And I want to thank all those who believed in me from the start. Without your encouragement, this couldn't have happened. Thank you.

One

The sun had set and the day faded away into the night. The stars and moon hid behind the dense cloud that veiled the sky above Toronto, hanging low and making the city seem that much darker for it. It was a Sunday evening, and most of the shops in the Westwood Plaza had already closed up for the evening. There were a few cars in the parking lot, scattered around in different spots, belonging to owners of shops still inside counting the day's earnings or reorganizing the stock for the next day.

The plaza was a small strip of eight stores including a hair salon and a laundromat, and two restaurants that closed early on Sundays. The little strip was dark and lifeless. A couple of neon signs had been left on while others were turned off by their owners or had never worked. The stores' windows were dirty, covered with a thin layer of dust that had blown over the glass during the day.

The parking lot had room for three rows of cars in front of the shops, reaching out towards a sidewalk and then the road. An alley stretched behind the buildings along the back with several dumpsters of varying size placed with no particular care. The lot backed onto a little park, so densely populated by trees it could have been designated as a small forest.

Along the west side of the building, parked on the path

connecting the front parking lot to the back alley sat a dirty white van, the kind of van that was a dime a dozen, seen all over the city, one nearly indistinguishable from the next. This one was very dirty. Almost purposefully dirty. The van's make and model were covered with mud, as was the license plate, preventing any real positive identification from being made, other than "a dirty white van." But this van was not dirty by accident.

"All right, we good to go?" asked a soft voice.

"Give it, like, five more minutes," an older voice said.

"You sure? We don't want the guy to leave, y'know. He'll set the alarm."

"Don't worry," said the older voice, a little gruffer this time. "I've scouted this for the last couple weeks. Sundays, he stays after he closes the store for an hour. I figure he's countin' money and shit like that."

"Or loading the gun," said a third voice.

"The guy is like eighty years old, he can't handle a gun," said a fourth voice.

"Oh, that's sound logic," said the soft voice.

"Shut up," the fourth voice replied.

"Both-a-ya shut up," said the old voice. "I doubt he has a gun, but even if he does, no chance he can get to it or get it out before we're on him. It's four-on-one."

"I had a night like that once," said the fourth voice. "Four, sexy—"

"Men. Yeah, we know," said the third voice with a chuckle.

"No, no. It was four sexy ladies, thanks."

"Yeah, and they were all on your computer screen," said the soft voice.

"Well, yeah. Who said it wasn't?" said the fourth voice with a wink, which could not be seen under the dark sunglasses.

"You two done flirting?" said the old voice impatiently. "Time to get to work."

"Okay, boys. Let's do it," said the third voice.

"Get in."

"Get the merch."

"Get out."

"Go."

The van's front doors opened and out got two men, one on either side. The driver was a very large man standing over six feet tall and four feet wide. He was a beast of a man, a huge bulk. He looked like a game-ready linebacker but he wore no shoulder pads. Out of the passenger side stepped a slighter man, tiny compared to the driver, but he was average all over. Average height, average build. He looked like any member of the public you might see. The side door opened and out climbed an athletic looking man. He had the build and gait of a gym trainer. His muscular legs tapered up to a smaller waist, and he slowly widened as over his chest and shoulders. He stood a few inches above six feet, and carried himself well. Behind him stepped out the fourth man. He moved quickly, despite his extra bulk, and ran around the front of the vehicle and climbed into the driver's seat. He was shorter than the other three but pretty thick for a small man.

All four were dressed the same: loose fitting black cargo pants, a gun tucked in the waistband at the back, and black work boots, black hooded sweatshirts fit loosely on three of the four men, but the largest of the four found his a bit snugger than the rest. Each man wore a dust mask and dark sunglasses, and a black toque with the sweater's hood pulled up over the toque. Their faces were painted black, and each wore thin white latex gloves with their shirtsleeves pulled over the cuffs of the gloves. There was no visible skin to indicate ethnicity. Their sizes and voices were the only things that differentiated them.

After the smallest of the group had got into the driver's seat, the three other men walked towards the third store from the end of the plaza. The huge man carried two empty duffle bags while the other two walked, hands by their sides. They reached the front door of Al's Jewels and Diamonds. Inside, the owner, Albert Schultz, knelt on the floor behind the counter, arranging stock in a glass display case.

Average stepped up to the door and knocked while the other two flanked him, standing on the far sides of the two windows that framed the door. The door and windows were barred to prevent break-ins. Average knocked on the door.

"Hello? Is anyone in there? My car won't start. Hello? Can someone help me?"

Albert looked up, closed the case he was working on, and locked it. He placed the basket of rings and necklaces on the floor behind the counter.

"Yes," he called back to the voice at the door, "just a minute." He got up from his knees and walked slowly to the door.

"Hello?" Average called out. "Oh, thank God," he said. "I thought everyone had gone home!" He backed up from the door turning back to the street, so as to hide his intimidating appearance.

"Not quite everyone," Albert chuckled. "Some of us

do still have work to do!" he said with a laugh as he unlocked the door and pulled it open.

"Well, bless your working heart," said Average as he turned back towards the small man inside. Average raised his leg and planted his foot in Albert's gut, kicking him down to the ground.

Average stepped through the door. His kick had sent the old man reeling back and crashing to the floor. Quick as lightning, Big and Athlete stepped through the door and closed it behind them. Average and Athlete reached behind their backs and pulled out their guns. Big stepped over to the counter where the register sat and put his duffle bags on top. He unzipped them and turned back to the other three men in the room. Athlete was pointing his gun at Albert as he walked around the store, looking at the rings, necklaces, jewels, and diamonds in the display cases. Average stood over the small man. Albert looked tiny and insignificant as the large figure stood over him.

"All right, pal," said Average in a deep voice that was not his own. "We don't want to hurt you. We just want the good stuff, the real good stuff, and we will be on our way. You can file an insurance claim and get your money back, and everyone walks away happy. You want to walk away, don't you?" Albert stayed silent and nodded.

"Good. So, let's get up off the floor," said Average, motioning with his gun, "and go to the back room safe. Open the register along the way!"

Albert nodded. He pushed himself to his knees and got up.

Athlete stood, ankles crossed, arms crossed but the gun still pointed at Albert. Big had not moved since he put the duffle bags down on the counter.

Albert stood up and froze for a second, not sure what to do. He had never been robbed before. He knew that owning a jewellery store could result in this sort of thing, but the store was in a good neighborhood. He was scared and hadn't been this scared in years. He thought of his wife, waiting at home, preparing dinner, expecting him home soon. But now he might not make it home. What if these men killed him? His hands began to shake, and he couldn't move his legs. He felt the pressure of the cold steel of the gun press against his neck. "Come on, old man, start walking," said the deep voice with a hint of impatience.

"Okay, okay," muttered Albert. He began to walk towards the opening between two counters so he could get to the back of the store. His knees shook as he took each step. The tall, thinner man stood on his left, tapping his foot on the ground impatiently. Albert looked up at him as he passed. He couldn't see any expression on the figure to his left. As Albert got close, the figure jumped forward and then stopped when Albert whimpered and put his hands up to protect himself. Athlete laughed at Albert's distress. Average shot Athlete a disappointed look, but since his face was hidden under glasses and mask, Athlete missed it.

Albert walked between the counters and turned right. There was an old revolver under the counter beneath the register. "I just need to get the keys for the lock," Albert said nervously, eyeing the gun tucked under the counter.

"Yeah, yeah. Get them."

Albert walked over to the register, lifted it, and reached under to release the drawer. It sprung open, and he stopped it with his hand. Big, who had turned, watching Albert the whole time, grabbed the register, and turned it around to face him. He started scooping out the money from the sections in the drawer.

Albert began to reach down under the counter, but he felt the pressure of the barrel against his neck, so he slid his hands over the handle of the revolver and into the little cup that held the keys he needed. The keys jingled as he pulled them out of the container and shook them. Average lifted the gun off of Albert's neck and shoved the old man towards the back of the store.

Athlete walked over to Big, leaned in close, and said, "This is easy, eh? Why didn't we hit this guy before now?"

"Shut it," Big said quickly and quietly as he shoved the last of the bills from the cash drawer into one of the duffle bags. Athlete walked behind the counter, looked to the floor and spied the basket of rings and necklaces Albert had been working with before they entered. He bent down and picked it up. He smiled behind his mask and reached over to the duffle bag Big had just filled. He dumped the contents of the little basket into the bag and put it back on the ground. He grabbed the second duffle bag and walked into the back room.

Athlete walked in and Average turned to look at him. He motioned with his head over at the open safe. He began filling the bag with bundles of cash.

Albert finished unlocking the last cabinet and stood up. He backed away and looked up at Average.

"There. I have done what you asked. Just leave me. Take it and leave. Don't hurt me."

"You did well. This will be smooth. Just come back out front with me and we will be out of here before you know it."

Albert walked in front of Average, moving too slowly for the younger man's liking, resulting in a couple shoves with the gun.

"Just kneel in front of the register with your hands on your head." Albert complied. Average looked over at Big, nodded, and Big walked around the counter, carrying the half-full duffle bag. Average stood over Albert, relaxed his gun, and crossed his arms. He leaned against the counter beside Albert, watching his two partners fill the duffle bags.

Albert was kneeling right in front of his gun. It was pushed to the back of the shelf, out of sight from the man standing beside him. Albert began to lower one hand, very slowly. The man took no notice of him. Too focused on his partners, thought Albert. He continued dropping his right hand slowly and reached for the gun. He felt the grip of the revolver in his hand, wrapped his fingers around it, and began to slide one finger over the trigger as he pulled the gun towards himself. He had the gun in his hand, hovering above the shelf, and began to pull it out when the glint of steel caught Average's eye.

"Oh! What the hell do you think you're doing!" yelled Average. He swung his arm around, resting the barrel of the gun on Albert's forehead. Albert, shocked, dropped the gun from his hands, and it landed on the shelf with a soft thud.

"Back up. Back up from there," said Average, motioning away from the counter with his gun.

"I'm sorry! I'm sorry! I...I don't know what I was thinking! Don't shoot! Don't shoot!"

Big leaned out from the back room, duffle bag in his hand, looking from the small, old man to the younger man. Albert cowered, hunched over on the floor as the large man

— *16* —

passed. Athlete came out of the back soon after with his bag by his side and gun in hand. He tucked his gun back in his waistband when he saw all was under control and walked out in front of the counter to join Big. The two men stood there waiting.

Average looked down at the old man and raised his gun arm. His hand, holding the gun, came crashing down on Albert's head, butt end first, and knocked the old man to the floor with a crunch. The man collapsed, unconscious as a small stream of blood trickled down his head from where the gun had struck him.

Average walked out from behind the counter. The three men walked out of the store and jogged back to the van that they had left running with the lights off. All three climbed into the back. The driver put the van into gear, and pulled forward, out of the parking lot and onto the street, off into the night.

Two

Traffic was brutal. Cars stood still, the lanes packed. When they did move, it was by inches at a time. According to traffic reports on the radio, a tractor-trailer had jackknifed, blocking three of the four lanes of the Gardiner Expressway just past Jameson Avenue. The road was starting to clear as the police and emergency crews removed the truck from the main lanes of the highway. The police shuffled cars along through one lane, then two, and, after forty-five minutes, three lanes. There was some small debris left on the road. Nobody had been hurt, but two cars had slammed into the trailer of the jackknifed truck. The drivers stood to the side of the road, talking to police officers and giving statements. Each looked stressed and exhausted: A woman dressed in a business suit; an older man in wrinkled clothes; and the truck driver, a middle-aged man in ripped jeans and a very worn T-shirt.

Steve looked at each person as he slowly drove past the accident scene, wanting to go faster, but limited to the speed of the car in front. Sometimes accidents were interesting to see, but ninety percent of the time it was a dented fender. Nothing to look at, so it was just a "move along" type of scenario. But people liked to see what other people were doing.

"That's a shame," Steve said to himself as he passed the

accident, into the clear, pressing his foot down on the gas pedal, picking up speed. Steve sat in his truck, radio on, not listening to what came through the speakers. He sighed, leaned his arm against the window and propped his head up on his hand. He was always tired from work but was feeling especially tired this morning after a long night. The traffic problems did not help to wake him up either. Moving slowly, or not at all, had lulled him into a napping state. He began to feel his eyes droop, shook himself awake, and sat upright in his seat, hands at the 10 and 2 positions on the steering wheel. He hit the controls in the door and lowered both front windows, hoping that the wind whipping through the car would smash into his face and wake him up. It helped a little.

Steve continued his morning drive, hurrying but not feeling like he had to floor it between stoplights to make up time. He was not eager to get to work. Construction was gruelling and when you were tired, it was even worse. He pulled off the highway at Spadina and went north. Traffic was still slow, but Steve knew his way around Toronto, so when there was a holdup he took some side streets. He turned onto a side street and saw, up ahead, a McDonald's. Steve chuckled to himself as he saw a reason to delay his arrival at the job site. He reached into his pocket and pulled out his phone. He clicked 3 and hit call. It rang twice.

"Hello?" said a gruff, old voice on the other end.

"Yeah, Frank, Steve. What do you want from McDonald's?"

"McDonald's? What're you doing there? Why aren't you here?"

"Traffic, truck accident, usual Gardiner bullshit. What do you want? Ask the other two."

He heard the voice grow faint then louder as Frank leaned away from the phone and hollered at his two co-workers.

"Ehh! Jack! Jacky! What you want from McDonald's? Coffee? Okay. Kev? You? Nothing? You sure? All right. Steve, yeah. Two regular coffees, two muffins. Get that deal they got there."

"Yeah, all right. Be there in, like, twenty."

"Okay."

Steve closed his flip phone ending the call. He drove into the parking lot of the McDonald's and manoeuvered into the drive–through lane. He pulled up to the speaker and leaned out of the window. The muffled, static filled voice greeted him and asked for his order.

"Three small regular coffees, and three muffins. Just, three different types of the muffins." The static-muffled voice repeated his order, gave him his total, and told him to drive to the next window. Steve pulled up to the window, handed the girl a ten, and cupped his hand waiting for his change. She dropped the coins into his hand, and Steve moved up to the next window. The window opened, the attendant handed him a cup tray with three coffees and three individually bagged muffins.

"And the juice?" asked Steve.

"Sorry? Juice?" said the man inside—"Josh," according to his name tag.

"Yeah, I had an orange juice?" Steve said. Josh looked at the receipt, puzzled as to why he didn't see a juice on it. "Did they forget it again? They always do. It's just a small orange juice," said Steve.

Josh looked up at Steve, looked out the window at the

line forming, and said, "Oh, okay. Just a sec." Josh turned to the beverage dispenser, filled up a small orange juice, and handed it to Steve.

"Thank you," said Steve, putting the juice into the cup tray inside his car.

"Thank you, sir. Have a nice day," said Josh, closing the window and turning away. Steve smiled and pulled away. He drove for another ten minutes, and arrived at the site . He pulled into the parking lot, parked beside the Honda Civic he recognized as Jack's, and got out of his truck. He popped his hard hat on top of his head, grabbed the drinks and muffins, and walked into the building.

Steve passed other workers along the way, nodding to them as he walked. Other demolition guys, plumbers, electricians, and site supers. The site was already pretty busy, but Steve was an hour and a half late because of the traffic, so of course, the work day had started without him.

Steve found his three friends and co-workers, Frank, Jack, and Kev, at the far wall of the building, smashing and chipping away at concrete walls with sledgehammers and chipping guns. Dust kicked up into the air as the concrete broke and splintered. The metal thrumming of the inner workings of the chipping guns echoed through the room battling for sound supremacy with the chisel end that smashed into the concrete over and over. At first, Steve only saw three workers, but as he got closer, he recognized each man individually:

Frank was the oldest and biggest. He was a huge man. He worked out but ate a lot. He had layers of fat and muscle that covered his body seamlessly and made him the overpowering figure he was.

Jack was tall and athletic. He worked out, played sports, and took care of himself. He was a bit of a joker and thought of himself as a ladies' man, and from the stories, he had told, and encounters the group had witnessed, he was probably right.

Kev was the smallest of the crew. He was a small man, but he was powerful. Steve was sure that everything that made up Kev was muscle, or at least it had to be because he was strong for his size. Steve fit right in the middle of the group. He was average height, build, and weight. He just looked like any other guy. There they were, the four of them: Big Frank, Athletic Jack, Average Steve, and Short Kev.

"Coffee!" Steve shouted. Frank turned and as Steve caught his eye, raised his hand in a slight wave. Steve responded raising his hands gesturing towards the men with the coffee and muffins. Frank turned to Kev and Jack, tapping them on the shoulders, and then turned back to Steve. Kev and Jack put down their tools. Jack wiped his brow and walked over to Steve, grabbing a coffee and muffin. Kev took his gloves off and joined the other three. He looked at Steve as Steve offered him the orange juice.

"I didn't ask for anything," said Kev.

"Yeah, and I didn't pay for it," Steve said with a wink.

"You didn't?" asked Jack. Steve replied with a smile and a wink. Kev smiled. "Thanks," he said, grabbing the juice from the tray.

"No problem," said Steve.

"I can't believe how often that shit works," said Jack, shaking his head.

"What?" asked Steve.

"Your juice scam," said Jack with a laugh, sipping his coffee. He removed the lid to let it cool.

"Ahh," Steve chortled, "yeah, well what do they care? It's not like it's the guy's personal juice stash," said Steve laughing and sipping his coffee.

"But don't they check the receipt?" asked Kev, sipping on the OJ.

"Yeah, but then they just figure it was an error, and they don't want to hold up the line, so what's a small juice? It only works when it's pretty busy. Otherwise, they have the time to double-check your order."

"Oh, of course. There is a certain finesse to it, isn't there?" said Jack, biting into his muffin, crumbs falling from his lips.

"Mhmmm," Steve agreed, his mouth too full of muffin to form words. He smiled, baring his teeth and all the mushed muffin stuck between them. Jack closed his eyes and turned away, washing down his mouthful of muffin with a swish of coffee.

The four men stood finishing their coffee, then Frank reached into his pocket and pulled out his cigarettes. "Toss me one?" asked Jack. Frank frowned at him, pulled out one cigarette, and threw it at Jack. He caught it against his chest, cupping it carefully with his hands so as not to break it.

"Thanks," he said. Frank grunted and tossed Jack the lighter after he had lit his own cigarette. Frank coughed as he exhaled the smoke.

"So we still taking down this wall?" Steve asked, waving his hand to the partially demolished wall in front of him. It was an interior wall, used to separate a small office in the back corner of the building. They had begun work on demolishing the wall the previous day, cutting and separating it from the rest of the structure.

"Yeah, me and Jack are gonna work on it," Frank said, taking a long drag to finish his cigarette. He rubbed out the butt against the concrete wall and tossed it to the ground.

"And me and Kev?"

"Well, you two can work on that front foyer window and doorway. The whole thing has to come out. Take the saw and start cutting." Frank instructed.

"The whole thing?"

"All of it. Take out the glass in the windows first, take off the doors, cut the seals along the walls and top and take out the whole frame. They want to replace it with a new one," Frank explained.

"Chu gottit," said Steve, faking a Spanish accent for no apparent reason. Frank shook his head as Steve and Kev turned to go to their work. Jack looked at Frank, "Which do you want?" he asked, gesturing to the sledgehammer and the chipping gun.

"Gimme the gun," said Frank. Jack picked up the gun, and leaned down, picking up the sledgehammer for himself. Frank turned the gun on, and began to chip at the concrete wall as Jack began pounding away at the wall with the hammer a few feet farther down.

Steve and Kev walked across the room. They walked beside each other but Kev moved closer so he could speak to him clearly. The building was filled with noise from drills to saws. Men shouted at each other, metal clanged against metal, and concrete smashed against concrete.

"So last night went pretty well, eh?" Kev said to Steve, quiet enough that nobody around would hear.

"Yeah, man. Good haul. Like, twenty grand or so? I think."

"Yeah. And went smooth, except for your close call."

"Nahh, he wasn't getting that gun out. Well, yeah he got it out, but he wasn't going to shoot it," said Steve. "Even if he did get it out, he was like a hundred, the force of the shot would've blown his own head off."

"Yeah, that's how guns work. He was right beside you, right? Point-blank, no matter how old, recoil or not, you're getting shot and probably killed!" Kev said in a harsh whisper, barely raising his voice but making his point very clear.

"Nah, I'm fine. I'm always fine. I had my eye on him."

"So how did he get the gun at all? How did it go so far?"

"I dunno, maybe I just wanted to make him feel good, like he had a chance or something."

"You better not be slipping."

"No. No, I'm not slipping."

"Like, I know the past few jobs have been easy and smooth but they don't always go like that, y'know. Shit does happen. We try to avoid that by planning and being careful."

"Yeah, I know. Relax! It's all good. We got away with it, nobody got hurt!" Steve said.

"Except the old guy you cracked over the head."

"Well, yeah. But that's small potatoes," Steve said with a chuckle.

"Small potatoes?"

"People say it. It's a thing."

"Yeah, maybe a hundred years ago," Kev trailed off.

"Whatever, man. Let's do this shit!" Steve said, pumping

his fists as the two reached the hallway with the doorway they had to remove.

The hallway was twelve feet high, eighteen across. At both ends were identical doorways. Aluminum construction with windows and doors. The glass was wired so as to prevent break-ins. The aluminium was painted black and the silver handles of the doors glimmered in the light. The paint was scratched and peeling and the rough grey aluminum was breaking through as though it repelled the paint. The door-ways were dented through years of careless use by amateur movers unable to realise something didn't fit through the opening. The wire-mesh glass was cracked in some spots.

The two men looked over the doorway, looking at the glass and doors, to see how it was all installed, so they would know what tools were needed for dismantling. They went outside to Frank's van to get the tools they decided on: a concrete saw with metal blade, box cutter knives, a drill, impact driver, and a sledgehammer. They returned several minutes later and set to their task.

Throughout the morning, they cut away at the sealant around the windows and removed the glass, proceeding to cut the sealant between the concrete wall and aluminum frame. They unscrewed the hinges and removed the doors. They set all the pieces aside and began to work on the frame itself. It was assembled in pieces, but the seams had been welded, so they picked their spots and began cutting.

With the exchange of the blade, the concrete saw turned metal saw was deafening, and as the blade sliced through aluminum, sparks spewed out into the room shooting past whoever was cutting. The sparks never really did any dam-age other than a sting if they hit skin, and there was never any real fear of the sparks starting a fire. There was no accelerant anywhere so they just hit the floor and burned out.

The morning passed and turned into lunchtime, when the entire site stopped. Every worker had thirty minutes or so to eat everything in his lunch pail and have a cigarette if he was a smoker. Thirty minutes and dozens of cigarettes later, everyone got back to work, some workers returning to their task while finishing off a last bite of food, or taking the last few drags of a cigarette as they walked around the site.

By mid-afternoon Kev and Steve had removed all the glass and the doors from the frame and had cut along the outside of the frame on one side. The frame was bolted into the concrete wall and the easiest way to remove it was to just cut through the aluminum and bolts. They began to cut the parts of the frame where the windows used to be. They cut across the middle of the frame from one side to the other, splitting it in half. Steve smashed the bottom half of the frame, where the left window had been and it began to bend forward as he applied pressure. The metal was stubborn and was not going to break easily.

"She's comin'," Steve grunted, as he kicked into the frame, bending it some more. Kev stood back, arms folded, watching his friend kick and stomp the frame.

"Oh yeah," Kev said with a smile, "She's goin' down as easy as your girlfriends." Steve looked back at Kev, pausing as he did, and laughed.

"But not as easy as your mom! Ahhahahaha!" Kev shook his head and laughed. The metal frame bent more and more under Steve's weight.

"Here we go, here we go!" Steve said, as he felt the metal give more and more. It was now bent at a forty-five degree angle. "This should do it," Steve said. He grabbed the frame at shoulder height. There were two columns: One framed the window and the door, while the other framed two windows. They were cut off at the bottom but were still well connected to the ceiling. Steve grabbed the two columns and used them as handles. He stepped up onto the bent metal and lifted himself and dropped down with as much force as he could muster. The metal bent but did not give. It shrieked lightly.

"Ahhh, there we go," Steve said looking over at Kev for acknowledgement. Kev nodded in agreement. The metal would surely give out with one or two more drops.

Steve lifted himself and repeated the drop. The metal bent and groaned under the pressure and weight of Steve's body. He lifted himself again and gave it everything he had. He landed hard on the metal. It creaked, groaned, and snapped at the bottom, smashing forward and clattering onto the cement floor. Not expecting the metal to snap so easily, Steve lost his footing. His feet slipped forward and out from underneath him. His hands slid down the aluminium columns as he lost his balance. He released his grip and threw his hands back behind him trying to balance. His feet flew forward and parallel to the ground, his upper half followed his legs and Steve went crashing onto the ground lying on top of the metal he had just broken. He lay there for a second not moving and then broke into laughter. Kev watched the whole ordeal in what appeared to him as slow motion, and hunched over laughing, gasping for air. A few workers nearby heard the crash and looked over, laughing to themselves as they pieced together what happened.

"Holy shit!" Kev exclaimed between breaths. "Are you

all right, man?" he asked Steve.

"Ohhh, man," Steve groaned. "Yeah, I think so." He sat up and rubbed his lower back, the impact point of his fall.

"That was ah-mazing," said Kev, drawing out the last word.

"Well, I'm glad you liked it," Steve said, groaning.

Frank came over, having heard the commotion. "What happened?" he asked. Kev explained to Frank what happened, and Frank laughed as he called Steve an idiot.

"Well, I dunno 'bout you guys, but I need a fuckin' beer tonight!" Steve shouted at his friends. "All right," Steve said, looking at Kev, "you can do the other side."

"Eh, sure," said Kev. "Well, now that I know what not to do, should be a piece of cake."

The rest of the frame came down without incident. The remainder of the afternoon was used to remove the frame and cut it into smaller parts. Steve had asked Frank what they were doing with the frame, and Frank said the frame was scrap. The project managers didn't care about it. It was trash to them.

"That means it's ours for the taking?" asked Steve.

"Yep," said Frank. "Put it in your truck and take it to the scrapyard. Should be a few hundred bucks."

"Chu gottit," said Steve. He and Kev cut up the metal scraps, loaded his truck, and took it to the scrapyard Frank had directed them to go to. They returned forty minutes later with a nice little sum of money. Steve split it into four and gave a portion to each of his co-workers. They were a close-knit bunch. They had worked together for a couple of years in construction and extracurricular activities. They got along well on the site and in the bar. They had fun together and trusted each other with their lives.

Steve and Kev had gone to school together and been friends since grade four. They stuck together through high school, and both decided to work instead of trying some post-secondary education. They worked a few small jobs here and there but moved into the construction world through a mutual friend who set them up with a job. On their first construction job they met Jack, who was a year younger, and they became good friends. The three worked together, and from that first job they began to wander along the darker path after talking to Jack. They began their extracurricular activities, and through one of those jobs, they met Frank. Jack had worked with Frank a few times before and introduced Kev and Steve to him. The four got along well from the start. Within the next year, the four had established their relationships and were a crew. They kept it small and clean, nothing too big that would draw a lot of attention. They each watched crime shows and knew the basics of what to do and what not to do. They were careful and happy to split the profits of each job. Frank usually brought in the most ideas and targets. He liked to go for drives to scour targets so that he got out of his house and away from his family because, as he said, they would kill him well before any robbery-gone-wrong would.

Trust is a key part of a robbery team. When you trust each other, everything goes well. You can focus on your task and get the job done properly. When you can't trust the people you work the job with, you are always double-checking each other, checking your back, and looking over your shoulder.

The first few jobs they pulled were a little rough as

they got used to how each man worked. They ironed out any problems so that the next job would run perfectly. They had not been caught, and no one had done any time. They were clean, without any police history other than speeding tickets or parking tickets.

The construction jobs gave them the tools they would need for the heists and access to areas without suspicion. Construction is incessantly taking place all over the city, and a white van with construction workers hanging around was not suspicious. They blended in until it was time to act. By then, routes had been scouted, routines observed, and disguises made. Through their jobs, they made connections with sellers and suppliers. They sold their goods for money and bought supplies for the next job. There was never any record of any transaction, so both sides were clean. Moving their acquired merchandise was easy. They hid it in tool boxes, crates, and bins from sites. To any passerby, a transaction would look like dropping off construction tools or supplies.

As the workday drew to a close, the building emptied and the site cleared. Plumbers and electricians had left by three o'clock, due to union regulations, and the site supers had left before lunch for meetings. They rarely ever came back, unless there was a problem. If they had anything to say, they usually called someone on the site. Jack, Kev, Frank, and Steve were the last ones to leave. They closed up the fence and locked it for the night.

"So, beers?" asked Steve. "I need some healing medicine," he said, rubbing his back as he hunched over, embellishing his soreness from his fall earlier that afternoon.

"Well, I don't wanna get home just yet," Frank said

with a smile.

"Gotta check in on our favorite waitress, don't we?" said Jack.

"Aww, yeah!" The other three said in unison.

"The Foxhound it is! See you boys there!" Steve said as he climbed into his truck.

Three

The Foxhound was an old-fashioned Irish pub. The crew liked to go there once in a while for a few pints and a good time. They walked in through the front door, the large wooden slab creaking as they opened it, and stepped onto the wooden floor. It still had a sheen from its new days, but when the light glanced off the floor, the scuffs and scratches from the hundreds of patrons showed on the planks. The floor creaked in spots, which gave the place an old-timey feel. It was a homely pub, opened back in the early 1980s by an Irish immmigrant who had borrowed money from the bank. He wanted a place of his own, a business to run and support his family, but he didn't want to leave Ireland behind, so why not open up a pub? He took ideas from all the pubs he'd wandered through in his youth, and made his own in Toronto.

To the right of the door were a few steps to take you to a raised section with several booths and floor tables, and a forty-inch television mounted on the wall. To the left were six four-seater tables, and a couple of smaller twenty-inch televisions angled down from opposite corners of the ceiling. Straight ahead was the main room. Booths lined the left side, and tables lined the right, while a handful of tables sat in the centre of the floor. It was arranged so that the aisle to the back of the pub was wide enough to accommodate two patrons walking side by side. Along the back wall and curving along the right side of the room was the bar, all wood from the counter to the stools that lined it. The header over the bar came out as far as the bar itself, with wooden inlay and simply carved features. It looked old-fashioned, but that's what gave the place its charm. Although, to keep with the times, the televisions behind the bar were LED flat screens, because not everything old-fashioned was good for business. The place wasn't huge but could easily accommodate a hundred people.

The crew walked in the door, workboots clacking on the wooden floor. Steve led the way with the rest following behind, pocketing their packs of smokes and lighters, Kev unzipping his jacket, and Jack pushing his hair to one side, out of his face.

"Man, I hate that you can't smoke in these places no more. Like, don't they know an honest man wants a beer and a cig after work? Don't they know we work hard and just wanna sit down with a beer, enjoying some nicotine?" Frank complained as he dropped his pack of Du Mauriers on the floor. "Shit."

"Stop whining, man. Every time we come in here, or anywhere, you gotta bitch about not smoking indoors. You need the extra exercise walkin' outside and back," retorted Steve.

"I ain't fat, man. I don't need exercise, I could be in those Strongman competitions. I'm not fat, I'm powerful," replied Frank, as he got up from one knee, cramming the pack of smokes into his left pocket, exhaling hard as he stood up with a groan.

"Listen to you, man! What thirty-four year old groans

like that getting up from one knee?" Steve snapped back, stopping as he half-turned to watch Frank struggle to get up.

"He's right, man," said Jack. "You sound like those old people in infomercials. You know the ones where, like, they got those chairs that go up the stairs 'cause they can't go up the stairs, so they use that chair to go up the stairs. Those old people stair chairs that go up the stairs. You know what I mean? I saw it on…"

"Yes! We all know what you're talkin' about, moron! After the third description, we just got it," Kev said, stopping Jack mid-sentence.

"Yeah. He's like that. Frank, you sound like those old peo—"

"Fuck you, Jack. I got it. And same to the rest of ya. I may be a bit older than you guys but I seen more, been through more, and can still do a helluva lot more than you can," Frank said.

"Yeah, if it was eatin' sandwiches," Jack muttered to Steve who smirked. The four sat down in a booth that was made to hold six. Kev and Steve sat on the inside seats, while Jack and Frank took the outside. Frank plopped down into the seat with a whoosh of air escaping as he did. The other three looked at him with wide smiles, ready to remark, when he looked up at them disapprovingly with tired eyes. "Yeah, yeah." The other three chuckled.

The pub wasn't too busy tonight; a few booths and several tables were taken, and two guys sat at the bar. A couple of minutes after the guys sat down Becky, the server, came over to greet them. "Hey fellas, how we all doing tonight?"

"Well, I know I'm a little better now you're here, love,"

said Jack, angling his body towards her, subtly flexing his arm that rested on the table. "Charmer as usual, eh?" Becky said, looking him in the eyes, but using peripheral vision to notice the flex.

"Only for you," Jack said with a wink.

Steve and Kev exchanged a look and shook their heads. Becky smiled, and Frank stepped right in, "Oh yes, dearest, I feel a lot better now you're here, 'cause I'm ailing for some ale, and I know you have it, so enough with Jacky-boy here and how about you get some beers?"

"Hey, now," said Jack, turning his head towards Frank but leaving his body pointing at Becky, "no need to be so mean to such a pretty girl! She doesn't deserve that, just 'cause you're sad 'cause you're old."

"I'm not ol—" Frank said, stopping mid-word with frustration, but letting the anger subside as he realized he did owe an apology. "Sorry."

"Thank you," said Becky, "but no worries, big guy."

"That's better," said Jack. "Now, the old man there will have a prune juice, room temperature," Jack told Becky. "The cold hurts his dentures." He whispered the last part loud enough so that Frank heard. Frank gave Jack the look of death. "I'm just kiddin', man! No need to get all red in the face." Frank unclenched his fists and retracted the laser beams. "We'll just get a couple of pitchers of Coors Light?" Jack asked his friends, looking around the table for acknowledgment of his choice. Each nodded yes.

"Two pitchers of Coors. Three glasses and a sippy-cup for the baby," she said nudging Jack and looking over at Frank, winking. Frank smiled back and Becky left to get their order.

"You really think she's buying all the BS you're selling?" Kev asked Jack.

"Whether she buys what I say or not, it doesn't matter. What matters is the playful chit-chat we have. It slowly breaks down her guard, and we continue to talk, flirt, and one day she will give in. Sometimes it's easy, but there's nothing wrong with a challenge, or working for something. And, come on, look at that ass," Jack said turning his head towards Becky, whose back was facing them as she took the order of the couple at the table on the opposite side of the room.

All four guys turned their heads to look. Becky stood there, in the relaxed position, one leg forward a little more than the other, right hip pointed outward as she rested her weight on her right leg. Her tight yoga pants caressed her legs, which were clad in black boots just below the knee. The drawstring for her folded apron rested on top of her firm round cheeks. Her long, lean legs rose and widened to her hips, and then she slimmed out again. Her not-too subtle curves were accentuated by her clothes.

"Damn, I love those yoga pants," Jack said. Kev nodded, eyes not breaking away from Becky.

"I would do…things, man," said Steve, "such things."

"Mmmmhhmmmm," Frank said as he licked his bottom lip, staring at Becky.

"That's creepy, Frank. And you're married," said Kev.

"So what, kid? I can still look, just can't touch. On purpose. But accidents do happen," Frank said, with a wink and a chuckle. Jack smirked, Kev looked at Frank with disgust, and Steve kept his gaze on Becky who had just finished taking the order from her new customers and turned to walk back to the bar. With the show over, the four guys returned their focus to the table and each other.

"So, the other night went pretty well, eh?" Steve said to the trio sitting around him.

"Yeah, was pretty smooth, no real problems," Kev said.

"Well, yeah the operation, procedure, went well, but we need a bigger haul, man," said Frank.

"But we're just doin' small-time stuff, big guy. I don't wanna get caught," Jack replied.

"Stick to what we know, what we can handle," Steve said.

"Yeah," said Frank, "but we can handle more, man. We been doin' this small-time stuff for a couple years now, never been caught."

"No, never been caught, but a few friggin' close calls!" Kev said to Frank. Jack and Steve nodded, agreeing with Kev.

"Yeah, but we are careful, we have the tools, we have the means, we just gotta find the right target," replied Frank.

"Well, I dunno, man, I think we are doing ok for now. We got enough income to maintain ourselves, right?" Kev asked. Steve and Jack nodded, Frank tilted his head to the side with a shrug.

"Could always use more," said Jack. "Some of these girls expect a nice dinner and stuff."

"Yeah, but the usual calibre of girls you go for are happy with fries and a Coke from some grease pit. And you're cheap enough to only offer that much," Steve said, nudging Jack as he spoke. Frank leaned back in his seat and let out a bellow.

"Well, they might not be full right after dinner, but trust

me," Jack said, looking at each of his friends, "I fill them up with dessert." Jack raised his eyebrows up and down, leaned back, folded his arms over his chest, and smiled a big smile, closing his eyes to think back on his numerous sexual conquests.

"Sleaze bag," said Kev.

"Maybe," said Jack, "but it's how I roll. Back to business, all I'm saying is that there is nothing wrong with more money."

"Fuckin' A," said Frank and Steve in unison.

"Jinx! One-two-three-four-five, you owe me a Coke!" exclaimed Steve, catching Frank and the other two off guard.

Frank looked at Steve disapprovingly, "What're you, fuckin' ten? Shut up with your 'jinx.'"

Becky arrived with a tray, rested it on the table, and took off the two pitchers of beer and the stacked pint glasses. "Here you go boys," she said, "anything else right now?"

"Uhhh," Jack muttered, looking around the table. "What you guys wanna eat?"

"Nachos?"

"Wings."

"Fries."

"One of those platters?"

"I'll give you guys a few more minutes to figure it out," Becky said with a smile. She turned on her heel, stopped for a moment, and then walked away.

"See that!" Jack said quietly to the others, "she did that little turn for me."

"What the hell are you talking about?" asked Kev.

"Yeah, she knew what she was doing," said Frank, "but it wasn't aimed at you, it was for me."

"The old man? No chance," Jack said with a snort.

"She did it on purpose, that little turn and pause, pushing her ass out," Steve said.

"She was just turning to leave!" Kev exclaimed.

"How blind you are," said Jack with a disapproving look towards Kev, who squinted his eyes and twisted his mouth back at Jack.

"They do work on tips," said Steve.

"So there you go," said Jack. "She wants more money, so she does a little extra. Just like we should," he said bringing the conversation back to business.

"Yeah, okay pal," Kev retorted, "sticking your ass out for a couple extra bucks is one thing, but committing a crime and raking in huge amounts of money are completely different!"

"Maybe," said Jack.

"Nah, it's the same," said Frank. "If she can do it, so can we."

"Well Frank," said Kev, "go ahead. I think you could get quite a lot of money if you stick your fat ass out a bit."

Jack and Steve burst out laughing.

"Fuck you," Frank said, as he cocked his fist and slammed it into Kev's shoulder.

"AAAHH! Fuck man!" Kev cried out, clutching at where Frank made contact. He pushed the big man back. Frank didn't budge and just laughed at Kev's pathetic attempt.

"All right, all right, calm down you two," said Becky, who had just stepped back in front of the table. "So what'll it be? You guys reach a decision after that?"

Jack looked up at Becky, reached for her hand and said,

"I am so sorry you had to witness such a disgusting display from these animals. You should not have been subjected to such barbarianism."

"Big word there, Jack," commented Steve. Jack threw him a look and then turned back to Becky with soft eyes.

"Yes, it was truly frightening. Thank heavens you are here, Jack, to comfort me," Becky said sarcastically.

"I'm here for you, sweetheart," Jack said with a smile. Steve piped up from the back of the booth, "Pardon my interruption of the love birds, but I think we'll get nachos and the party platter with medium sauce on the wings?"

"Yeah that's good," Kev said.

"Okay with me," said Jack.

"Do it up," said Frank.

"Thanks, boys. I'll be back!" Becky turned just like she had before, aiming a little more towards Jack this time, and walked away.

"I told ya," said Jack with much satisfaction, "I told ya." Frank laughed, Steve stared blankly out after Becky, and Kev just shook his head in disbelief.

The front door of the bar opened and in walked a young, scruffy looking man. He wore jeans, Converse trainers, and a light jacket that swayed open as he stepped forward revealing a Ramones T-shirt.

Jack looked up and over Frank's shoulder towards the door, seeing the man walk in, and said to the group, "Oh, look who decided to show up." Kev turned around to look, Steve looked over the booth, and Frank made an attempt to turn, groaned, and faced forward again.

Matthew hesitantly stepped forward, moving slowly into the pub as he scanned the room looking for his co-workers. He spotted the booth and the men looking towards him. He lifted his head sharply in a "hello" as he made eye contact with Jack, who returned the gesture. Matthew approached the booth and when he arrived, stood in front of the table. He looked at Frank, who looked back and said, "Not a chance, Junior." Matthew looked over to Jack who looked up at him, exhaled with a groan, and then got up out of the booth to let Matthew in. He slinked in and Jack sat back down beside him. The booth was now full.

"Didn't think you were going to make it out, Junior," said Frank, leaning back from the table.

"I said I was coming. It just took a little longer to get here because of the traffic."

"Well, we already ordered, obviously," said Frank. "We weren't waiting for you."

"Wouldn't expect anything less from you, Frank," said Matthew. Becky walked over to the table with a fifth pint glass. "For the new guy," she said and then walked away.

"Thanks!" Matthew called out after her.

"So where the hell you been today, kid?" Frank asked Matthew.

"Today was my class day. I've been working with you for, like, five weeks, and you still don't know that I go to class on Wednesdays?"

"No, I knew," said Frank, trying to cover up his memory lapse, "I meant, like, what did you do at school, 'cause you usually finish early enough that you shouldn't have been late. Right?"

"Yeah, true, fair enough," Matthew agreed.

"Got yourself out of that one, Frank," whispered Kev, leaning towards the big man, but whispering loud enough that the rest of the table heard.

"So, what were you up to?" asked Steve.

"We had a field trip downtown," said Matthew.

"Seriously?" asked Frank, "They still do that? Hah!"

"Yeah, they do…" said Matthew. trailing off and taking a sip of beer.

"So, where did you go?" Kev asked.

Matthew straightened his back, sat up, and said, quite academically. "The Thomas Fisher Rare Book Library."

"Yeah, that sounds like a school trip. Nothing fun anymore these days," said Jack.

"It was actually not too bad," said Matthew. "I thought the same as you," he said pointing at Jack, "but it was pretty interesting. They have, like, tons of these old books. Like, decades, and some over a hundred years old. The librarian guy there had a bunch out on display in this room, and we got to check them out. He explained a little about each of them, some history and how they made were made. Then we got to examine them, check them out."

"Like, touch them and stuff?" Steve asked.

"Yeah. I was surprised. Figured they would make you wear fancy gear or something to examine them, but nope. Just couldn't touch some of the ink on the pages of some of them. And you have to be careful so you don't rip or ruin anything."

"Oh, well, no shit," said Frank, taking a big gulp and finishing off his glass.

"Yeah…" Matthew said, dragging out the end of the word. "There were some cool old scrolls and stuff, but the best thing was probably this Shakespeare book. Well, not a book, what did he call it? A folio! Yeah, a Shakespeare folio."

"And I'll assume it's an old copy of a Shakespeare play?" asked Steve.

"Well, yeah, sort of. It's like an almost original collection of a couple of plays. It was huge too, like this," and using his hands Matthew showed the group the width and height of the book, which was about fourteen inches wide, eighteen inches tall, and four inches thick.

"Damn. That's a big book," commented Frank.

"Yes, Frank. How perceptive of you," Matthew said dryly. "But that's not the best part," said Matthew half sarcastically, eyes widening. "The folio was acquired by the library at an auction for—well, how much do you think?"

"I dunno, like, a thousand bucks?" said Frank.

"Noo, gotta be more than that," said Steve, "I'll say like a hundred thousand."

"What?!" Frank cried out. "No way, it's still a book. Can't be that much." Matthew sat quietly with a grin on his face. Frank looked at him. "Can it?"

"Two hundred thousand," said Kev. "No, wait, three hundred."

"I'll say, one dollar, Bob," Jack said laughing. The rest chuckled.

Smiling, Matthew looked around the table. "Well, actually, it went for six—oh!"

"Here we are boys, platter and nachos," said Becky, appearing from nowhere with a plate in each hand. She placed each on the table. "Anything else right now? Another pitcher?" She asked, leaning over the table to pick up the empty jug. Kev looked at the table, Jack smiled and stared straight ahead at the chest that lowered in front of him, as did Frank. Steve stared right down her shirt, caught himself, looked up, met Becky's eyes, and then nervously kept raising his gaze up to the ceiling, putting a quizzical look on his face as though he was in deep thought. Becky smiled, knowing she'd caught him and leaned back.

"Yes please, another pitcher of the same if you could," Frank said.

"Right away," and Becky turned and paused, knowing each guy would be watching her.

"Damn, she's hot," said Matthew.

"Fuck sakes, she caught me," Steve said shamefaced. The rest stared at him, jaws open and eyes fixed, mimicking him.

"Well, I don't think it was that bad," Steve said, reaching to the plate nearest to him for a handful of nachos.

"Yeah, she's fine, she's got a full figure. What about this book? How much did it go for? You were saying six something?" asked Frank.

"Ohh yeah. Right. Ummm, it went for…" Matthew said, dragging out his answer as Frank leaned forward anticipating the response.

"Yeah? Yeah?"

"Ohh, right. Six million."

"Get the fuck outta here! Six million? Are you serious? Six million?!" Frank exclaimed loudly with incredulity.

"Dollars?" Jack asked.

"Of course dollars, you idiot!" snapped Frank. "Holy fuck," said Frank with disbelief. "Six million dollars. For a book."

"That's pretty incredible," said Steve.

"Yes sir," said Matthew, satisfied that he blew the minds of his friends. "That library is pretty damn exciting now, isn't it?"

"Do they have lots of books there worth that much? And you can just go and touch them and stuff?" Frank asked.

"I assume so, yeah, but he only showed us the one, and he stood there watching over it as we looked at it."

"They must have, like, armed guards or something there. With stuff that valuable," said Kev.

"Nope," replied Matthew, "nothing like that at all."

"What?! How is that possible?!" Frank cried out.

"I dunno, but that's how it is. Maybe there's, like, crazy laser grid trip alarms like in the movies," said Jack.

"Yeah, maybe. I didn't see or ask or anything. It was just cool to see something like that," Matthew said.

"Yeah," said Frank quietly, "maybe, maybe not." He looked up and caught Steve's eye. Steve noticed that Frank was thinking hard. His faced was scrunched up and his brow furrowed. Steve wanted to ask him what he was thinking, but he had a feeling he already knew.

"These nachos are pretty good, eh?" said Matthew with his mouth full, some salsa trickling out of the corner of his mouth, down his chin.

"Yeah, not bad at all. But I have an appetite for something else tonight," said Jack turning his head and nodding towards the bar where Becky stood pouring a pint.

"When do you not have an appetite for that?" Kev laughed, as three of the others joined in the laughter. Frank mustered a little chuckle, but was still distracted by his thoughts.

The pub had filled up pretty well for a Wednesday night—the Leafs were playing and that usually brought in a bit of a crowd. The boys paid attention to the game, but their focus was on their table. Frank was lost in thought for a while about Matthew's story. The guys went back to their usual conversation about stuff they'd seen on TV, girls they knew, had been with or wanted to be with, and old work stories, with the occasional bursting cheer as something happened in the hockey game that was playing on the television with the audio blasting through speakers. The guys were laughing after Jack told Kev about Frank smashing his shin with a hammer earlier that afternoon.

"How do you manage, Frank?" Matthew towardsasked.

"Did you ever hear of Jacky's little experience about a year ago or so?" Frank asked Matthew.

"I dunno. I don't think so," replied Matthew.

"Oh, well then, kiddo, you're in for a treat," said Frank.

"Okay, so what went down?" asked Matthew. Kev and Steve chuckled and sat back, knowing what story Frank was about to tell. Jack leaned back, looking a little nervous, not sure which of his escapades Frank was about to share, but as Frank started to talk, laughed out loud himself, realizing which story it was.

"So, like a year or so ago we were working on the renovation of this community centre, right in the middle of 'Rainbow Town' downtown," Frank started.

"Rainbow Town?" Matthew asked.

"Yeah," said Frank, "y'know, like beth't dreth'd part of the thity" Frank said, sticking out a flat hand and bending it straight down at the wrist.

"Ohh, you mean like, gay town?" Matthew asked.

"You're quick, Junior," Frank said.

"So, it was a gay community centre?"

"Yeah," said Jack, "it was totally into other dude buildings, especially that CN Tower," he said with a wink. The whole table laughed.

"Right, so we were working in this gay community centre," Frank continued, "and when we started we were told that the building isn't totally closed down, so there are gay people walking around the place, but not really in the construction areas. So Jack here decides that he needs to go to the bathroom." Jack nodded with a straight face, and Matthew began to smile.

"So, he goes off down the hall, and we keep working," Frank said, gesturing to Kev and Steve.

"Building benches or something, right?" Kev said.

"Yeah, I think so," said Steve, "I remember lots of wood around." The table chuckled.

"So, Jacky there goes down the hall to take care of his business, and about a minute after he's gone, we hear like, heaving and nasty sounds, sounds of a guy throwin' up. We stop, look down the hall, and there's Jack, hunched over, pants around his ankles, one hand on the wall just heavin' his guts out. I don't even know what you ate, but I think you ejected dinner from the day before. It was nasty, man," said Frank, laughing. Steve and Kev were laughing, struggling for air as they remembered the event, Jack had a smile on his face as he sipped from his glass, and Matthew laughed but still had a puzzled look on his face.

"So what was it, Jack?" Matthew asked. "Did it just reek horribly in there or something?" Jack looked down into his glass and shook his head no.

"Oh no, it wasn't a smell. More of a sight," Frank explained. Matthew smiled, looked over at Jack, who was still trying to hide in his glass, looked over at Kev, hunched over the table, laughing into his arms, looked over at Steve, arms folded and leaning back laughing, and looked at Frank for the explanation.

"A sight?" Matthew asked.

"Oh yeah. A sight," said Frank.

"What was it?" Matthew asked with anticipation.

"Well, when Jack opened the door and walked in, half unzipping his pants so he could get right down to business, he accidentally stumbled in on two other gentlemen," Frank said laughing, barely getting the last few words out before he burst out into a great bellow of a laugh. A smile crossed over Matthew's face, while his brow furrowed, still not quite getting what had happened to poor Jack.

Matthew turned to Jack, "So? Usually, there are other guys in a public bathroom." "Yeah," said Jack, "but usually one isn't bent over the counter while the other one feeds it to him from behind!" Jack shouted back at Matthew, as the rest of the table hollered and laughed, slamming the table with hard fists, almost knocking over their beer and sending some nachos flying into the air.

Matthew broke out into laughter louder than the rest as he finally understood the perils Jack had faced.

"It was something else man, totally not for me. The second I saw them, my stomach turned over and everything came up, I got the hell outta there so fast, just turned and left and started yakking all over the floor. It was fucked, man. They didn't even stop or slow down when I entered. And my pants were already unzipped," Jack continued, "so when I saw them, I was so shocked I lost my grip, and they slid down to the floor, and the one guy that was on the counter looks over and winks," Jack explained, head still down in his glass. He took a big swig and then chuckled to himself. The other four guys were crying at this point, barely breathing from laughing so hard. "I can still picture it…" Jack trailed off, frowning into his now empty glass. He had started the story with the glass full.

"I'm sure you still picture it often, Jacky," said Frank, laughing.

"Oh yeah, all the time," Jack said, his words dripping with sarcasm.

"It was amazing!" Kev added.

"Truly fantastic!" Steve chimed in.

"Yeah, Jacky-boy found two soul mates!" Frank said, in a mocking dreamy voice.

"Oh shut the fuck up!" Jack said to the table, but with a smile on his face.

"I never want to see that again, man. It was rough," said Jack.

"Poor Jack, banging all the girls, but can't handle a couple of fellas goin' at it. Not that there's anything wrong with it!" said Frank, quoting *Seinfeld*. The table burst into a fit of laughter again.

The minutes passed as every drop of beer emptied from the pitchers into the glasses, into the bodies of the patrons, and out into the bathroom. The exciting life of a lager: constantly in motion. Not every drop made it to its intended target. Some were lost with hard clashes of "Cheers," sloppy patrons spilling from their glasses, or from big sloshes and swigs that dribbled out the sides of mouths, trickling down chins and dripping onto tables, napkins, and hands alike.

"All right, I gotta go," said Matthew.

"Already?" asked Kev.

"Yeah," Matthew confirmed.

"Kid's got a bed time!" said Steve laughing.

"Gotta be home, or you're in trouble, eh?" asked Frank, taking a big glug from his glass.

"Yeah, plus I'm friggin' exhausted," said Matthew tiredly.

"All right," said Frank, "Usual time tomorrow, same site. Nothing's changed."

"Okay," said Matthew. He got up out of the booth, reached into his wallet, pulled out a twenty, and threw it on the table. He slapped hands with Jack, Steve, and Kev, and patted Frank on his large shoulder. "Have a good night, guys," he said and walked to the exit.

"What a bitch," said Frank, "Like I don't need sleep. I'm still here," he said grumpily.

"Yes, and we love you for it," said Jack sarcastically. "It would be so terrible without you," Jack said laughing.

"Fuck you," said Frank as he reached for another chicken wing from the platter in front of him.

Quite a few more people had walked in since the beginning of the night, and the bar was full of hockey fans watching the Leafs.

"They won't win," one man said to another.

"They're on a streak, though! Four wins!" was the reply.

"Yeah, but they're gonna blow it somehow. They always do."

"Nah, man. They got this! They're fourth in the conference!" The other man responded with a wave of his hand, returning his attention to the game on the TV above the bar.

Minutes later, cheers broke out through the bar as Auston Matthews buried his twenty-first goal of the year with a beautiful snap shot from the half boards. High-fives were exchanged between fans and cheers rang throughout the bar as new conversations picked up on the hot streak Matthews was having.

Jack turned to his friends, "He's ripping it up, eh? What a shot!"

"He's a beaut!" said Steve, in his best Don Cherry voice.

"They're doing well this year. Could be the year," said Kev.

"Oh yeah, and I'm happily married," joked Frank.

"Well, you will be when they win it all. Cup's comin'," said Jack.

"You're so delusional, Jack. Just like with Becky there. 'Oh, that little ass pose was for me.' Fuck you," Frank said, imitating Jack and laughing as he cursed him.

Jack just sat back and smiled, "You'll see."

The game continued, the Leafs continuing to score, just staying ahead of the goals from their opponents that night, the Boston Bruins.

The guys ordered another two pitchers and some more wings to last them until the end of the game. They finished off their food with a few minutes left in the third period, the Leafs leading 5-4.

"Come on, you rich sons of bitches!" Kev yelled at the television. Time ticked away, the Leafs held on to their lead, and the bar exploded with cheers as the game clock ticked 00:00.

"Fuck yeah!" cried out Jack.

"Whooooo!" yelled Kev and Steve, one after the other.

Even Frank joined in with a yell and a clap.

"I told ya," said Jack.

"Yeah, yeah," said Frank. "Well, the money they get paid, they better friggin' win."

Becky came over to their table just after the game finished, still looking as good as when her shift started, asking the boys if they needed anything else.

"Just the bill, sweetheart," Jack said to her. Becky returned a few minutes later, and the boys all chipped in to pay the bill. They got up from the table, put on their coats, and walked towards the door, all turning to give a goodbye to Becky.

"See ya later, boys!" she called out to them. Each returned with a "bye," or a "see ya," except Jack, who turned to her, gave a little tip of the hat and a wink. The boys left the pub, gave each other fist bumps and handshakes and went to their respective cars to head home for the night. Frank got into his big white work van, Jack into his Civic, and Steve and Kev into Steve's Chevy truck.

Four

Frank drove his van home along the side streets, taking the long way back, hoping that when he arrived home and stepped into the house, everyone inside would be asleep. He could just go to the kitchen, get a glass of water, head upstairs, change, and slip into bed. Unfortunately for Frank, that is not how it went.

Frank pulled into the driveway, seeing through the front bay window that the lights in the kitchen were on. "Dammit," he muttered to himself. He put the van in park, opened the door, and stepped out with a groan. He was tired. His body ached as it usually did after a long day of work, but a little less today because of the beers he had polished off at The Foxhound. He walked slowly towards the door, each step feeling heavier than the last, hoping that the lights would go off so he could attempt a silent secret entrance, but to no avail. He opened the door and stepped inside.

His wife, Jessica, looked out from the kitchen. "Where the hell have you been?" she said in a harsh tone. She stepped out of the kitchen, leaned against the door jamb, and folded her arms across her chest.

"The girls are asleep?" Frank said, craning his neck, gesturing up the stairs.

"Yes, sound asleep. Where the hell have you been? It's almost midnight!"

"Can't I just get in the door and take my coat off first?" he said, as he pulled his right arm out his jacket. He reached for a hanger from the closet, hung up his jacket, and turned back to his wife. She looked at him from the doorway to the kitchen, raised her eyebrows, and asked her question again, this time with a hand gesture, opening her hand as though waiting for something to be placed in it.

Frank sighed and frowned. "I went for a drink with the guys after work. I told you I was going to. I called." Frank explained to her, as he sat on the stairs taking off his work-boots.

"A drink does not take five hours, Frank. And since when are we able to go for drinks all the time, huh? Did you forget about your daughters?"

"No, what do they have to do with this? I went so that I could have a social life. I like to go out, you know. I don't want to be stuck here all the time." He said as he stepped towards her.

"Oh, so with us you're stuck, eh? We aren't good enough company?" She turned and walked back into the kitchen. Frank followed her in.

"You know that's not what I meant. Just take it easy! Work is tough and I need to relax. You know it can get crazy 'round here sometimes."

"Yeah. Of course, I know. I'm the one who deals with it all the time. I swear, Frank, it's like you have telepathic powers and you know when there is shit going on at home, and then you just don't come home 'till it's all done. All taken care of. By me!" she shouted at him, slamming her hand on the counter.

"Jessica, if I had powers I wouldn't be here. And we

would not be struggling. We'd be fuckin' rich, livin' in some mansion where it's warm, Florida, or something like that."

"Sure, Frank," she said, crossing her arms, looking at him, disappointment written across her face.

"Look, I don't want to fight. I'm exhausted and I just want to sleep. It's late."

"Mmhmmm," She said, drawing out the end of the word, showing her frustration with him.

"Look, I know it's tough. We have two girls, and I love 'em to death, but they're a pain in the ass, and a cost we are barely covering. It's not easy with you out of work right now, so I have to try to do as much as I can with the construction. I'm bringing in as much as I can, but if I don't go out once in a while, I'll kill someone," he said, a joking smile across his face as he finished. "I love you, babe, you know I do."

"I love you, too. But sometimes it's a chore being married to you. I don't know if we are going to be okay next week, let alone next month," she said with a huff and brushed past him, obviously still upset with him. He turned and grabbed her arm.

"Money is a little tight, but work is going well. We are busy with projects, and the money will come in. Don't worry. I might pick up a couple side things from some guys I know too. We will be fine."

"Well, I'm sure you are creating some great ideas down at that fuckin' pub you live at." Jessica turned away from him and went upstairs to the bedroom to get herself ready for sleep.

"I don't get it," Frank muttered to himself. He ran his hand through his thinning hair, sighing heavily as he did so.

"You try to do everything you can for them, but they still fuckin' hate you."

He poured himself a glass of water, sat down at the kitchen table, leaned back, and sipped his water slowly. Several glasses later, he went up to get ready for bed. Jessica was already lying in bed, eyes closed, drifting off. He looked around the room, his master bedroom, although, many times it felt like he didn't even belong here. Some sweaters and jeans from previous days were draped over a chair in the corner. The bedside table had a couple of old magazines on it, the corners curled from having been read so many times during the restless nights when insomnia from worry kicked in. He often sat up wondering how to get through the next day, and how he was going to get his family through the next month. He looked at his wife, lying in bed, so peaceful. This was how he liked her. Quiet. He smiled to himself, knowing that this peace never lasted.

Frank tried to be as quiet as he could, but he was a big man and made bumps and thumps without trying. He sighed as occasional snorts from his wife followed his accidental noises. He changed from his day clothes into some pyjama pants and a tank top he picked up off the floor, right where he left it that morning when he changed into work clothes. He went to the washroom, washed his face, and stood in front of the mirror, leaning close, looking at the life fading from his eyes. They used to sparkle, but that was long gone. His face showed the life he now led, one of fatigue and frustration. He rubbed his eyes, saying to himself, "I gotta do something. I can't keep this going." He shut off the light, walked across the room, the floor creaking under his bulk, and climbed into bed.

Back at the Foxhound, Steve got into his truck and unlocked the doors so Kev could climb into the passenger seat. They buckled in, and Steve slid the key into the ignition, turned it, and the engine of the truck roared to life. He flicked on the headlights and pulled out of the parking lot onto the road. Kev didn't live too far from Steve, so it was easy to pick him up and drop him off. Kev had a little car, but occasionally the two drove each other, taking turns.

"Fuck, I don't want to work tomorrow, man," Kev said to Steve.

"Yeah, I know what you mean. It's such a fuckin' chore to get up at, like, five a.m., drive there, and start work at, like, six. Such a pain," Steve replied.

"I never used to look forward to weekends so much. Even back in school, y'know? Class was always a bitch, but this is worse. But what else is there? It's ridiculous finding a job out there, and there is always work here," said Kev, leaning on his hand that rested on the door. He looked out the window at the passing cars and buildings. People on the streets heading home, to friends' places, late night stores or bars.

"Yeah, it's a steady paycheque," Steve said.

"I want to be like these people, not a care in the world. Just wandering the streets, no urgency, just living life," Kev said, keeping his eyes out the passenger window.

"Must be nice to be those people. I just want enough money to be happy, y'know? Not have to worry if I can make the next payment on the car, or my rent, phone bill, all that shit."

"Yeah. Just to go out and chill with your buddies, like we did tonight. Have enough stuff to do to keep you busy, but not stressful."

Steve pulled up to the curb in front of Kev's building and put the truck into park. "Well maybe one day. Until then, back to the fires of hell tomorrow, bright and early."

"Heh," Kev chuckled, "Yeah, maybe one day. Until then, I have my escape. Good 'ol Xbox." Kev smiled, and Steve returned a smirk.

"Later, Kev."

"See ya, man." Kev got out of the truck, closed the door and turned with a wave. Steve put the truck into drive, did a quick three-point turn, and drove off into the night. Kev walked to the front door of his building, swiped his keycard across the reader, heard the door unlock with a metallic *ka chunk,* and opened it. He walked into the little vestibule, opened the second door and walked up the stairs to the third floor where he lived.

Kev had a little apartment in Kensington Market, enough for himself. One bedroom, one bath with a combined kitchen and living room. The tiny little bedroom fit a bed, and not much else. Kev had spent most of his money furnishing his living room, making it the perfect gaming room. He was a gamer at heart and lived in that room. The other rooms were stops along the way. The bedroom was for sleeping, bathroom for the bath, and the kitchen was for cooking. Kev spent as little time in the other rooms as possible, maximizing his gaming time.

On the wall hung a forty-inch LCD television with HDMI cables flowing from the back and sides. Power cords and standard AV hookups were intertwined with the mess of cords as well. Below the television was a small TV table, the kind that normally holds a television set, but Kev had used it to set up his video game devices. The newer consoles took the spotlight—Xbox 360, PlayStation 3, and the Wii U, but in behind was the Wii, and PlayStation 2. Just below the tabletop was an opening meant for VCRs and DVD players, but Kev had his original Xbox set up there. Below that were two doors. Inside were the Sega Dreamcast and Genesis, and the original Nintendo and Super Nintendo. Kev was proud of his collection of gaming consoles and occasionally turned on the old models for a nostalgic play-back of some classics and favourites.

On the right wall of the room were several shelves that held and showcased all the games Kevin owned. He had thirty-five Xbox 360 titles, twenty-five PS3 titles, ten Wii U titles, a CD wallet of all thirty Wii games he had—they were burned copies because Kev had modded his Wii him-self to try to save some money on games, twenty Dreamcast games—a combination of legit and burned, twenty Genesis games, and forty NES and SNES games. There were a cou-ple of original Xbox games on the shelf, but most of the games he had for it were burned onto the Xbox's hard drive itself because Kev had modded that console for free games as well.

On the left wall were posters of his favourite games, *Metal Gear Solid*, *Call of Duty* and *Gears of War*. Kev was a fan of shooter games. Across from the television was a re-clining chair, black fabric with black stitching. It had a little fridge built into the side of it where Kev kept some Powerades and energy drinks for those extra-long gaming sessions.

Kev walked into his apartment, took off his shoes, threw his jacket on the floor, and went over to his Xbox 360. He turned it on, plopped himself into his chair, turned on the TV, grabbed his 360 controller and headset, tuned them both on, and settled in. Kev selected *Call of Duty: Modern Warfare 3* and started up the game.

"Just a couple of games before bed," he said to himself. He loaded up the multiplayer, started a game, and began play. He stayed up for two hours, playing over a dozen games, shouting at the TV and other players over his mic, working himself into frustration. But such was the gaming lifestyle. After Kev had lost two games in a row towards the end of the second hour of play, he decided to turn in for the night. He shut everything off, stripped down to his boxers, and climbed into bed. He set his alarm to wake him up in four hours and drifted off to sleep, still going over that night's epic matches in his head.

❖

After Steve had dropped Kev off, he headed home, stopping along the way to fill up on gas. He drove with The Offspring's latest CD playing at a pretty decent volume. Steve sang along to the lyrics he knew and trailed off on the ones he didn't, humming or singing the beat when he didn't know the words.

The drive home took a little over twenty minutes because of the stop he made for gas. He arrived at his apartment, parked his truck on the street in front, grabbed his lunch pail from the back seat, and locked the truck. He walked to the front door of the building, waved his key card over the magnetic reader, and opened the door. He walked into the elevator and rode up to the seventh floor.

Steve's apartment was not much bigger than Kev's, but it was much more of a home than a place to crash. Steve had furnished it properly with a futon and chair in the living room, meaning there was room for guests. He had an HD TV, a PlayStation 3, mainly for its Bluray use, and a cable box. Steve was much more of a television and movie person than a gamer, but he had a few games to go along with his PlayStation. He walked into his little kitchen, put his lunch pail on the counter, opened the fridge, got out some mustard and shaved ham from a couple of days ago, and took out the bread from the cupboard. He made a sandwich, put it in a Tupperware container, and put it in the fridge. Then he got out some cookies, put them in a container, and put them in his lunch pail. His lunch for tomorrow was ready.

Steve walked over to the futon in "couch mode," as he liked to call it, referring to it as one of the Transformers because of its ability to change shape, and sat down. He flicked on the television and flipped through the channels until he found *The Tonight Show Starring Jimmy Fallon*. He laughed along with the jokes and skits until he began to feel sleep sneaking up on him. Steve's eyelids were dropping down. He closed his eyes several times, almost drifting off before he caught what was happening to him.

"Well, might as well just sleep," he said to himself. Steve groggily turned off the television and walked to the bedroom. He changed into some soccer shorts he had from the days he used to play and went to the bathroom. He brushed his teeth, flossed, and checked himself out.

"Not bad," he said to himself, smiling. He walked over

to his bed, pulled back the covers and slid in. He pulled the covers up to his chest and closed his eyes. But they did not stay closed. His mind began to wander, back to the pub, to the stories, and to Becky's fantastic body. He felt a bit uncomfortable as the mental image of her sharpened and, lying in bed began to raise the sheets.

"Oh, fuck sakes," Steve muttered, "when I'm tired and want to sleep. Always when you don't want it to happen." Steve slapped his tent, but that only made it more rigid. "Well, if you have to, you have to." He got out of bed, went to his laptop, opened it, and opened his browser. He then opened an "incognito" browser window so he could browse his sites without recording a history, but wondered why he did so since he lived on his own and nobody else used his laptop. He opened a few sites he liked and began to tire himself out. Steve got caught up in the heat of the moment and didn't prepare himself for the end. As he felt it come, he struggled to keep himself loaded with his left hand squeezing hard but not moving otherwise, while his right hand fumbled for the tissue box on his left.

Why the fuck do I put it on that side? he thought to himself. He reached the box, put his fingers inside, and found it empty.

"Ahhh fuck," he said, turning back to the screen. He looked down, throbbing in his hand, looked back up to the video in which the two ladies had not stopped while he struggled to hold back.

"Ohhh Fuuckk," he grunted and released tension, spilling onto his hand, legs, and down to the floor. He moaned with disappointment and satisfaction. He cleaned himself off with that day's boxers, climbed back into bed with a smile on his face, and fell asleep, still thinking of the two girls in the video he just watched.

❖

Jack got into his Civic, turned the car on and began searching. He checked the glovebox, the drawer under the passenger seat, and the little nooks and crevices on the dash. He checked the storage container between the seats and after several minutes came to the conclusion that he had no condoms. He sat back in his seat, looking forward, out of the front of the car towards the pub. The door opened, and a tall man in a blazer stepped out, raised his left hand to his mouth, rested the cigarette he was holding in his fingers between his lips and dug around in his pockets for the lighter. He found it after the third pocket check, brought it up to his face, and lit his cigarette. The glow of the lighter lit up his face until the flame went out and all Jack could see the man was his dark silhouette, smoke rising from his head and the occasional glow from the end of the cigarette as the smoker sucked and inhaled.

Jack gave courteous nods as he saw his friends drive out of the parking lot, on their way home. He turned up the radio, as the DJ introduced the next song to be played. It was some house or trance mix Jack had heard before. He liked it, drumming his fingers on the steering wheel to the beat. He exhaled with a sigh and put the car into reverse. He backed out of the parking spot, and threw it into first and pulled away. He left the parking lot, cracking his window a bit as he did to feel the cool night breeze brush against his face and through his hair. He left the little plaza the pub was in and drove down the street, through a couple of inter-sections until he came to a Petro-Canada station. He pulled into one of the spots in front of the little store, and parked. Jack got out, locked his car, and walked in. He walked to the back corner and started looking at the limited selection of condoms available. He picked a pack of three, walked over to the wall fridges, and picked out two Red Bulls. He only wanted one but there was a special if you bought two, so he indulged to take advantage of the deal. He walked up to the counter, put his items there, leaned back to look at the selection of gum on the shelves below the counter and picked some Excel Polar Ice.

"Gotta keep fresh," said Jack to the attendant. The attendant just looked at Jack and continued to ring up his items on the register.

"Petro-Points card, sir?" said the man, in a thick Indian accent.

"Ah, yeah," said Jack, fumbling through his wallet looking for the card. He found it tucked away and slid it across the counter. Jack kept his eyes down in his wallet, feeling through the few bills he had. Two fives and a ten, mixed among several receipts.

"Thirteen seventy-seven for you, sir," said the attendant, whose name was Peter, according to his name tag, but Jack did not believe that was his given name due to his thick accent.

Jack handed the man a five and a ten, only looking up as far as the name tag. The register beeped and responded to Peter's touch.

"One twenty-three your change, sir. Thank you."

"Thanks, man," said Jack as he grabbed his items, Red

Bulls in one hand, condoms and gum in the other, "Have a good one." He turned and walked out the door to his car. He placed the cans on top of his car, reached into his pocket for his keys, and opened the door. He sat inside, closed the door, and started up the car. He threw the gum and condoms into the storage container between the seats that was meant for CDs and realized he left the drinks sitting on the roof of the car. He opened the door and got out, keeping his head down as he called himself an idiot for forgetting they were up there, grabbed the cans, sat back inside, placed the two cans in the two cup-holders between the seats and closed the door. He put the car into reverse and drove back to the pub.

As he pulled into the parking lot, he looked towards the front door of the pub and saw his soon-to-be passenger. Becky stood, leaning against the wall, with her hands in her pockets. Her right leg bent up, foot against the wall while the left leg stretched down to the ground. She saw Jack pull into the parking lot, pushed off the wall with her right foot, and walked to the curb. Jack pulled up in front of her and leaned across to the passenger door to open the lock. Becky opened the door and got in as Jack was leaning back into his seat.

"Well, where did you go?" asked Becky.

"Just down the street to Petro, needed to get condoms," replied Jack, looking her in the eyes, smirking as he said "condoms."

Becky buckled her seatbelt and looked back at Jack saying, "You couldn't wait for me and then go?"

"I didn't wanna make you wait. I knew you were going to be a little while, so I figured I could get it done in time."

"Well, that didn't work, I was waiting anyway. For ten

minutes."

"Ten minutes ain't that bad. I'm here now, and we don't need to stop on the way. It's all good," said Jack as he pulled out of the plaza onto the street. "Your place or mine this week?"

"I believe it is my turn to host," said Becky matter-of-factly.

"Your place it is," said Jack with a smile.

The two had been having these late-night rendezvous for a couple of months now. It was meant to be just no-strings-attached fun, once a week or so. Jack had gone into the pub one night by himself when he knew she was work-ing, a few weeks after the group had met her at one of their pub nights, and slowly worked his magic on her. There was immediate attraction between the two when they first met. That night, Jack replaced sleep with sex, as he often did. There had been no real problems with their arrangement. The two were careful and took all the precautions of safe sex, though they did experiment and try new things.

"I don't understand why you don't just get the bigger boxes from Shoppers Drug Mart or something. WalMart probably even has them," Becky said looking at Jack with a quizzical look.

"I can't do that. I can't get those big boxes. It's weird and awkward when you buy those things," Jack explained. "I get uncomfortable when I go up to the cashier with those things. I tried once; it was way too awkward."

"You were embarrassed to buy condoms?" Becky stated. "You. You are uncomfortable buying big boxes of con-doms?"

"Yeah, so what!" Jack said defensively. "I can't even

make eye contact with the cashier when I'm buying them. It's just uncomfortable."

"You…you get uncomfortable buying condoms."

"Yeah! Why is that so hard to believe?!"

"Ummm, Jack," Becky said, with the same sarcastic tone she had been using, "you consider yourself a 'playa,' mackin' all the broads you can," she said, attempting a male voice for the last part.

"Yeah, I am. You know it, don't deny or hate."

"Mhmm," Becky said, cocking an eyebrow, "and you do all kinds of things to girls, talkin' to anyone with no shame, and yet, you get embarrassed buying condoms. Wouldn't buying a big box of them be like a trophy for you?"

"I dunno. Not really. It's just weird. The cashier looks at you like, 'oh you think you're getting laid, do you? Oh, look at you, off having sex while I have to fuckin' work.' It's just awkward to go through that," Jack explained.

"If you say so, Jack."

"I do say so. You don't know; you're a girl."

"The fuck does that have to do with it? I buy condoms. Not often, but I do, and I have no problem going to Shoppers to get a big box of them."

"Well, good for you," said Jack with some frustration.

"And wait a minute," Becky said as the car pulled up to a red light.

"What?" Jack asked, looking at her with a tired expression on his face.

"You say that you don't like buying condoms because it's awkward. Okay, I can understand that. You don't want to get the big boxes because it's uncomfortable at the check-out counter. Sure, whatever you feel. So, instead of getting the big boxes, you go to gas stations and get the little three packs that last you like a day."

"Yeah, and?"

"Don't you end up buying condoms more often? Because you get the smaller packs? Don't you run out faster and then have to buy them more often?"

"Uhh," Jack said, looking back to the road as the light turned green.

"Which means you have to go through more of your awkward feelings when you buy the small packs. So really, you're just going through more of your awkward situations because you want to avoid awkward situations!" Becky exclaimed with excitement.

"Uhhh, I guess. Yeah."

"That makes no sense, Jack!"

"Don't worry about it. I get by," Jack said with a smile.

"I dunno about you sometimes," said Becky, shaking her head with a laugh. "You're lucky you're pretty," she said, looking over at him, sticking out her tongue. Jack looked at her, half frowned and turned back to the road.

"So what amazing condoms did they have to offer at the gas station?" Becky asked, emphasizing "amazing" with a sarcastic tone.

"Oh, just you wait!" said Jack with excitement. "I got some cool new 'Fire and Ice' ones."

"Oh, those? I've heard of those. They, like, heat up and cool down right?"

"I guess so. That's what I figure," Jack said. "'Cause, you know how, like, sometimes we're going along, and then I like to pull out and let the air cool my cock down. It's all wet and, you know, it gets pretty hot in there, so you pull out and let the air cool it, and then I stick it back in there, and it feels so damn good."

"Yeah I know. I don't feel any difference."

"Yeah, well maybe with this you will feel what it's like, 'cause I figure that this condom, through some magic lube, does that for me! So I don't have to pull out! It'll just be hot and cold in there! It sounds amazing!" Jack explained, getting more and more excited.

"Well, as long as you keep fucking me, you can wear whatever condom you want," Becky laughed.

"Oh, don't worry. I'll keep fucking you," said Jack, reaching over sliding his hand between her legs and rubbing up against her with his fingers.

"Mmmmm," Becky moaned, reaching her hand over and squeezing his bulge. Jack adjusted himself in his seat and pulled his hand back. "Awww," Becky said, forcing a frown, and then smiling as she squeezed him harder.

"Okay, okay," said Jack quickly.

Becky licked her lips and leaned over to him, whispering into his ear, "I'm getting nice and wet, Jack. All for you."

"Fuck yeah," Jack moaned. Jack turned onto a side street, ran a stop sign, and sped down the street. He made a right into a townhouse complex, another right down the lane, and pulled into the driveway of the third house.

Becky eased her hand off of Jack and leaned back into her seat as he put the car into park. They undid their seat belts, and Becky got out as Jack got out his pack of condoms and grabbed one of the Red Bulls. He snapped open the can and chugged half of its contents in one gulp. He took a breath and finished off the can. He wiped his lips and put the empty can back into the cup-holder. He let out a burp, trying to muffle it with his hand. He got out of the car, closed the door, locked it and walked to the front door of the townhouse, where Becky was just unlocking the door. She opened it, walked in and turned on the lights. Jack stepped in after her and closed the door behind him. Becky undid her coat and reached into the closet for a hanger. Jack threw his coat onto the knob of the door and opened the pack of condoms, stuffing them into his pocket. He turned to Becky, who just finished hanging her coat up, and grabbed her around the waist. He spun her, so she was facing him and leaned in, locking his lips against hers.

They shuffled along the floor, tongues fighting for domination. They twisted and twirled around each other, flicking forward and back. The two barely stopped to take breaths. Jack's breathing got heavier as they continued to kiss, shuffling towards the stairs. They reached the bottom step and Becky hit it with the back of her heel. Jack bumped into her, and she pulled her face away from his. Their eyes locked in a fiery, passionate gaze, Jack breathing heavy as he swallowed. Becky smiled, reached down, patted him between the legs, grabbed his hand and turned quickly up the stairs. She led him to her bedroom, pushing open the door as they got there. She let go of his hand and walked over to the far corner of the room to turn on a lamp.

Jack closed the door behind him and began wrestling with his T-shirt. He got it off and began to unbuckle his belt.

"Mmm, not so fast, mister," Becky said seductively, almost moaning it as she stepped over to him. "You have to undress me first," she said as she ran her hands up his stomach across his abs, around his back and pulled herself in, kissing him. She felt him grab her hips, pulling her into his body, pushing his now fully erect dick against her. She moaned as she felt him against her. Their tongues flicked at each other, their heads exchanging sides as they continued to kiss, making their way towards the bed. As they kissed, Jack lifted her shirt up over her head, pulling his head back so the shirt could pass between them. Their lips came back together as her arms raised. He lifted the shirt off her and threw it aside. She replaced her hands on his back, digging her nails in. Jack's fingers slid up her back to her bra. He undid the clasp with ease and pulled the straps over her shoulders. She shrugged forward, keeping her lips against his, never letting the kiss end and he pulled the bra off and tossed it to the floor. She felt his hands on her hips, sliding up her slim stomach, up to her breasts. They moaned in unison as he reached them, squeezing them between his hands. His hands were big, and her breasts fit them perfectly. He gently massaged her with his hands as they stood, kissing.

Jack then pulled away, looking down at her breasts. "Damn," he whispered. She smiled and looked down, grabbing his hands and pushing them into her breasts, giggling as she did so. They both looked up, staring into each other's eyes, and she nodded. He pushed her backward onto the bed. She bounced when she landed, and moaned, biting her lip as he bent over, grabbed her pants by the waist and yanked them down. He kept pulling them down, past her knees as she wriggled out of them. He threw them aside and began kissing her legs, making his way up to her thong. He slipped his fingers under the hip strings and pulled it down revealing her bare, glistening mound. He pulled the thong off, dropped it to the ground and began to rub her. She squirmed under him as he played with her tenderly, rubbing her and sliding his fingers inside.

She moaned with pleasure as he played her so expertly. She arched her back as he continued to finger her, kissing her while he reached down below. He kissed her lips, her cheek, down her neck and slid his tongue across her nipples. She got louder as he licked, rubbed, and squeezed until she burst. Her body shook, and Jack lifted his head, smiling. Becky opened her eyes, panting, pushed him up off her, and pushed herself along the bed. She sat up, undid his pants and roughly pulled them down. He stood, smiling, arms by his sides as she pulled down his boxes. He stood in front of her; she leaned back down. He grabbed her hips and pulled her close. He bent down, reached into his pants pocket, and pulled out one of the condoms. He ripped the package open, and she took it from his hands. She placed it on the tip and unrolled it down the length of his shaft. He smiled and pulled her hips close to him. He grabbed his cock with one hand and pressed it against her soaking wet mound. She moaned as she felt how big he was as he slowly pushed inside her. He grabbed her hips and began to thrust. He grunted, and she moaned.

Jack pumped as Becky squeezed her breasts, both enjoying every second. Several minutes in Becky looked up at Jack. The pleasure was disappearing from his face. She furrowed her brow as he continued to pump.

"What..is..it?" she asked between each thrust.

"Don't you…feel how…hot it's…getting?"

"Mmhmm, but it's not…that different…than before," she said as the thrusts began to slow.

"Fuck. It's getting…really fuckin' hot, Becks. What the fuck?! This is supposed to be Fire and Ice. Where the fuck is the ice!" Jack yelled. Becky moaned as Jack pulled out.

"Ahh fuck! Get this shit offa me!" Jack cried out, anguish in his voice as he fumbled with his cock, grabbing at the tip of the condom. He tried to pull it off, but the latex just stretched.

"Fuck sakes!"

Becky slid up to the edge of the bed and watched Jack stumble around the room. She smiled but felt concern for her sexual partner. "Just start from th—"

"I know how to take a condom off, thanks!" Jack snapped at her. Becky put her hands up in defense and pursed her lips. She sat on the bad as Jack fell to his knees and began to roll up the condom from the base. He continued to roll it with the same motion you might use getting the elastic off a rolled poster while pulling from the top as well. At last, after an agonizing two minutes, the condom snapped off. Jack threw it across the room, sitting on the floor with his knees bent under him, cupping his cock, rubbing it and trying to wipe off the lubrication.

"Ohh fuck! That was the longest two minutes of my fucking life." Becky laughed, "Hah, usually your two minutes go by like that!" She snapped her fingers as she finished.

"Fuck you! I think I burned my dick! What the fuck!"

"Awww, muffin," she said sarcastically. He looked up at her angrily. Jack sat fanning air onto his crotch. Beck slid her thong back on and went over to him.

"Don't touch it! Don't touch it."

"Okay, I won't." She hugged him and squeezed his

shoulders. "Go shower and wash it off," she said, holding back a smirk.

"Yeah. Okay." He got up and walked over to the bathroom. He closed the door, and Becky heard him turn on the shower. The curtains pulled back, and he stepped into the shower.

"AAAHHHHHHHH!" Jack yelled as he stepped into the shower, the steaming hot water crashing into his already sensitive skin. "Fuck sakes!"

Becky laughed as he heard him cry out. She put on a pair of shorts and a tank top and waited for him to come out. Ten minutes later he emerged from the bathroom, head hanging low and skulked over to the bed. He sat down and reached for his boxers which Becky had put, with his other clothes, at the end of the bed. Becky sat up on her knees behind him and massaged his shoulders as he dressed his lower half. She helped him put his top on and asked,

"So how bad is the damage?"

"Well, I don't think I'm fucking for a couple of days," he replied, gloomily.

"Aww, you'll be fine."

"Yeah," Jack agreed. "Fucking condoms." He got up and walked towards the door.

"Goodnight," he said to her.

"Goodnight, Jack. See you soon." She smiled at him as he half smiled back. He turned, walked out the door and left to go home and nurse his wounds.

Five

Jack arrived on the site the next morning and parked his car. He looked out the window and saw Kev and Steve at the back of Frank's van, sorting through the tools. The day was beginning, and the sun was lighting the site, casting long shadows across the ground as it peeked through trees and buildings. A few puffy white clouds drifted against the blue sky, only noticeably moving if you stopped and stared. There was a light, cool breeze. The weather report said that the temperature was supposed to be hotter than yesterday. It was unusually hot weather for October, and everyone just blamed it on global warming. Jack was not looking forward to the heat. He preferred heat in the bedroom, not on the work site. But after last night, Jack wanted nothing to do with heat for a long while.

Jack got out of his car, reaching back in to grab his hard hat. He popped it on and closed the door.

"Hey, boys," said Jack as he walked to Frank's van, turning back towards his car. He aimed his key at the car, clicked the lock button, and with a beep and flash of the indicators the car locked and the alarm armed. He turned back to his friends as he got to the back of Frank's van. Kev and Steve looked over at him, nodded, and returned to the tools in the van.

"You seen the Skilsaw?" asked Kev, climbing into the

back of the van, moving two-by-fours aside.

"Didn't we leave it in the job box inside?" said Jack, making reference to the giant toolbox they kept on-site.

"I thought we brought it out," said Kev.

"Nah, I told you," said Steve.

"Should be in there," said Jack.

"Yeah, all right," said Kev. He climbed back out of the van, grabbing a box of nails as he did. He dropped the box of nails into a bucket with a handful of screwdrivers, scrapers, hammers, and screws. He picked it up by the handle and began to walk towards the entrance of the building. Steve closed the back of the van, locking it as he finished. He jogged to catch up with Jack who was walking alongside Kev.

"Hey," said Jack, "Where's Frank?" he asked, just realizing that the big, gruff man wasn't around.

"Inside," said Kev, "talkin' to the super." As the trio walked towards the front door, they overheard shouting inside. They recognized one of the voices as Frank's. The three stopped and looked at each other.

"Well, he's pissed," said Steve.

"Yeah, no shit," said Kev.

"Okay, so, I'm not going in there just yet," said Jack.

"Yeah," agreed Steve, "I think we forgot something in the truck."

"Yeah," said Kev. The three turned and walked back to Frank's van. They stood there and waited. They saw a grey Toyota pull up, park, and out got Matthew. He jogged over to the van.

"Morning, guys," he said as he got to the back of the van where the three were waiting.

"How was the rest of the night? Leafs win?"

"Of course," said Jack confidently. "Like there was any doubt."

"Nice. Anything else happen? You guys stay out late?"

"Nah," said Kev. "Left after the game. I played Xbox for like three hours or something when I got home though. I'm fuckin' wiped."

"You idiot," laughed Steve, looking at Kev.

"You do anything after?" asked Matthew.

"Cranked one out and went to sleep," said Steve proudly. Matthew laughed and shook his head.

"How about you Jack? Nail any broads from the bar?" Matthew laughed as he asked.

"No. Nothin'. Went home," said Jack quickly, avoiding the retelling of his unfortunate encounter last night. He crossed his arms and looked away.

"Okay," said Matthew with confusion. He looked to the other two for answers, but they just shrugged. "So what're we doing out here?" Steve asked.

"Frank's in there yelling. We decided not to get involved," answered Kev.

"Ah. Good call," said Matthew.

They waited outside by the van for another ten minutes. They saw the plumber arrive and nodded to him as he walked by. The sun was rising slowly, but the temperature was rising faster. They could already feel the sweat forming.

"Fuck sakes. I'm sweating already and I'm not even doing anything," said Steve.

"Fuckin' heat!" shouted Jack angrily.

"I guess we should go in soon?" asked Matthew.

"Yeah, I guess. Let's go," said Steve. "I'm tired of waiting out here. It's cooler in there, right? Let's just get to work."

Kev groaned as he picked himself up off the bumper of the van he was resting on. He picked up the bucket of tools at his feet and began to walk. Steve locked the van and joined the others walking towards the building. As they got to the front door, Frank appeared in the doorway.

His face was red, and he had a very angry look in his eye. He walked as though surrounded by a barrier of fire that represented the anger he felt. His T-shirt was soaked with sweat. A dark triangle of sweat started at his neck and reached down to his belly, pointing down. Other blotches of sweat soaked the shirt in random spots.

"Fuck!" he yelled as he pushed open the front door. He looked up and spotted the four workers heading his way. He walked up to them.

"Matthew. Go home, no work today," said Frank sternly. Matthew looked back at Frank, complete confusion on his face. He turned to Steve, Jack, and Kev, and each returned his confusion.

"Huh?" mumbled Matthew.

"Yeah. Nothin' to do. Go home," said Frank.

"All right," said Matthew, still confused. "See you guys tomorrow. I guess."

"I'll call you," said Frank. Matthew stopped, turned back to the group. Frank was watching him while the other three stood with their gazes focused on Frank. Kev had dropped the bucket of tools by his feet. Matthew turned back and walked to his car.

"What's that about?" Steve asked Frank. Frank gave no

response. He kept his eyes on Matthew until he left. The car revved into life and pulled away.

"WHAT THE FUCK YOU? DUMB FUCKS!" yelled Frank. The three men standing in front of him shrank into boys. They each stepped back, shuddering under the booming voice of Frank. "You two!" Frank shouted, pointing at Steve and Kev. "What the fuck did you two do yesterday?" Frank asked impatiently.

"We, uhh," Kev muttered. Frank glared at him. Then turned to Steve who answered.

"We took out that doorway thing like you said," Steve answered with a shaky voice, stumbling over the words.

By now, Jack had taken a step aside to avoid the fire coming from Frank. He stood, watching the action in awe and confusion.

"Well, guess what, you morons?" Frank said angrily. He didn't wait for them to respond.

"You took out the wrong fuckin' doorway!" Frank shouted.

"What? Fuck off!" said Steve.

"What're you talkin' about?" asked Kev.

"The doorway. You took out the north doorway. It was supposed to be the south. How did you fuck that up?!" shouted Frank. "Didn't you look at the fuckin' plans?" Steve and Kev just stared back at Frank. "Fuck sakes!" Frank yelled, stomping his foot and turning away from his incompetent coworkers.

"Okay, so we took out the wrong one. What now?" asked Steve.

"Well, I get fucked is what happens now!" yelled Frank, turning back to face Steve. "I talked to the building planner, and *they're* going to fix it."

"Okay," said Kev. "So we're fine. It gets fixed, and we're all good."

"No. We're not *all good*. *They* are going to fix it. Not us, *they*," said Frank sternly.

"We're off the fuckin' project!"

"Wait, what?!" shouted Steve and Jack. Kev stood with his mouth open.

"What do you mean?" asked Jack. "We fired? All of us?"

"Yes!" replied Frank.

"Why the fuck all of us?!" asked Jack with confusion and anger. "They fucked up, not me, or you!"

"Yeah, but we work as a team, one company. So we're all done," explained Frank.

"Oh, fuck off," muttered Steve.

"So, that's why you sent the kid home?" asked Kev.

"Yeah," said Frank, now feeling more tired than angry. He wiped his forehead, collecting the sweat on his brow, and then wiped his hand on his shirt after looking for a dry spot.

"So what the fuck do we do now? We got any other jobs?" asked Jack.

"Nope. Gotta look now. But not much is going on, I don't think," said Frank.

"Fuck. Sorry, Frank," said Kev.

"Yeah, sorry, Frank," said Steve.

"Go inside, get our shit outta there. Pack it up," Frank said. Jack, Steve, and Kev walked away into the building to collect their tools that they left in the job box. Jack smacked the window of the doorway as he passed it.

Frank walked back to his van and sat on the back

bumper. *What the fuck do we do now?* he thought to himself. He reached into his pocket and took out his cigarettes. He sat one on the edge of his lip and lit it. He puffed out the smoke. Took a drag. Inhale. Exhale. He finished the cigarette in six drags and stomped out the butt as he threw it to the ground. He put another cigarette into his mouth and lit it. He continued to smoke as he looked out over the site, past the fence surrounding it and into the street. People milled about walking to their jobs or homes. The cool breeze felt nice against his skin. It blew over his damp shirt and cooled him. He felt his temper cool along with his body. He had just finished his third cigarette when he looked up towards the entrance to the building and saw Jack walk out followed by Kev and Steve.

Jack walked with some anger in his step while Kev and Steve sulked behind, heads held low. They had their hands full with sledgehammers, concrete saw, chipping guns, buckets, and power cords. They reached the van and Frank got up, tossed down his used-up cigarette, and crashed it into the ground with his boot.

Steve reached into his pocket, fumbled around, and pulled out Frank's keys. He unlocked the van with a press of a button. The van beeped, the lights flashed, and Frank walked over to the back doors and opened them. Steve walked over, put the tools into the back of the van on the floor, and hung the cords on the wall-mounted hooks. Kev and Jack followed suit, putting away their tools. Frank slammed the doors closed when they had put everything inside.

"All right, boys. Go home. I'll call you. Or look around, talk to people you might know for jobs, and call me," Frank said.

"Where you going now?" asked Jack.

"Going to check out some places, look for work," said Frank. He opened up his driver door and climbed into his van. He waved at the three men standing to the side. He started up the van, put it in reverse, and executed a three-point turn. He swung the van around and drove down the driveway turning out onto the street.

"Fuck, man," said Steve. "How did we fuck it up that bad?" he asked Kev.

"I dunno, man. Shit happens, y'know?" Kev answered.

"Yeah. Shit happens. Fuck sakes. Worst twenty-four hours," Jack muttered.

"What else happened?" Steve asked him as they walked towards their cars.

"Nothing," Jack said stepping slightly quicker. He opened his car and waved to his friends as he got in. "See ya," he said.

"Later," said Kev. Steve waved and got into his truck. Kev got into the passenger side.

Jack started up his car and pulled away.

Kev sat down in the truck and closed the door. It was a quiet drive home, and Steve pulled up outside of Kev's building and let him out. Kev waved and went inside his building, up to his apartment to play video games. They were his distraction from the reality he didn't want to face. And they worked.

Steve drove himself home. When he got there, he tossed his work clothes aside and took a shower. He stood with the water raining down on him. His head hung down. The water was crashing into his shoulders and running down his naked body. The water was warm and it soothed him, but only a little. "Fuck!" he yelled and slammed his hand against the wall.

Six

Frank drove off the site, leaving his friends and co-workers behind. He was still angry about what had happened, but the anger and rage were subsiding as he listened to the radio. His focus was no longer on the job they lost, but now on the job they must get.

He couldn't believe that Steve and Kev had messed up so badly. Didn't they read the plans? He remembered telling them what to do. He couldn't remember if he had told them which door frame to take out, but he was almost sure he had said south. Maybe he said north? Maybe he didn't say at all. He had checked in on their progress during the day and it all seemed okay. There hadn't been any site-supers on the site that day, and nobody else really knew what his team was doing. Nobody else was going to step in.

Frank was more angry with himself than he was with Steve and Kev. *They're just kids, I guess*, he thought. He drove with no real purpose. His goal was to get home, maybe make a mid-morning snack, and then collapse on the couch with the TV on.

He drove through the city, looking out the side window at the cars passing by and people walking up and down the streets. The city was busy. His mind wandered from driving. He thought about the house he was heading back to, the home he had made for his wife and daughters. He cared for them.

He loved them. He bought the house when Jessica was pregnant with Sophie. They had lived in an apartment together for two years after getting married. Frank saved for the house so that he could have a proper place to raise a family, but the mortgage was slowly emptying the bank account. Things weren't getting any cheaper and he knew that money had to come from somewhere. Getting fired did not help.

Frank had always been a family man. Even though he was tough as nails on site, shouting and cursing his way through the work day, when Frank got home, he became a loving father. He wanted his girls, all three, to have everything they deserved. But Frank had a short fuse. He was constantly stressed, and even though he loved his wife and kids, he found himself escaping them. He loved them when they weren't around, but felt frustrated when they were. Frank wanted to make a proper living so that he could support his family. He felt he had done a proper job thus far, but ask his wife and the answer would probably be different.

Frank looked out the window as he approached a stoplight. Crossing in front of him from left to right was a mother and her child. She walked behind the stroller, pushing it along. Inside, Frank saw a little face poking out from the blankets. A tiny, chubby hand reached into the air and waved. Frank waved his fingers back as he caught the mother's gaze. She looked at him with confusion. Staring into the truck trying to see if she recognized the face. She looked down to her baby, craning her neck around the hood of the stroller, and saw her baby waving.

She smiled, looked up at Frank in his van while she continued to smile at him. Frank smiled back. Frank watched her, remembering when Sophie and Denise, his daughters, were that young. It was not so long ago, but some days it felt like an eternity.

The car behind him honked its horn and startled Frank from his daydream. He shook himself back into reality and looked out the front of the van. The light had changed to green. He hadn't noticed. He cursed himself. He hated when people in front of him didn't move the second the light turned green. Now he was one of those people. He stepped off the brake and pressed down on the gas, pulling away and speeding up to leave his mistake behind. Frank drove out of the city and into the suburbs where he lived. He turned down the side streets, passing schools, seeing the kids outside playing. *Must be recess*, he thought. He continued on and turned onto his street. The lawns were all groomed and gardens bloomed. Trees rose up from the ground into big green bushes of the sky. It was a picturesque neighbourhood, just short of the white picket fences. He pulled into his driveway and parked his van on the left side.

His wife was out somewhere and the girls were at school. Frank had the house to himself. Normally he would be happy to have his house empty, but today, after the moment he shared with the baby and mother at the traffic light, he was feeling nostalgic. He longed for the days when he and his wife cuddled on the couch, newborn Sophie curled in their arms. And later, when Denise was born, the four of them sitting on the couch, close and snuggled together. But as his girls grew up, he knew that those days were gone.

Frank got out of his van and walked up the path to the front door. He got the newspaper out of the mailbox, tucked it under his arm, and fumbled for his keys to open the door. He slotted the right one into the lock and turned it. The cool air of the air conditioning reached out and grabbed him, pulling him into the house. Frank took a deep breath of the cool air and stepped inside. He pulled off his boots by stepping on the heels. He walked into the kitchen, tossed the newspaper that was still tucked under his arm onto the counter, and walked to the sink. He got himself a glass of water and walked into the living room. He sunk into the couch with a groan and took a long drink of his water. He sat there, staring blankly in front of him.

Frank sat motionless, staring at the wall opposite him and occasionally drinking from his glass of water. To anyone who saw him, he would have looked as though he was asleep with his eyes open. But inside Frank was working. His mind was racing through the day's events, through the night before. He calculated paycheques, bills, expenses, and costs. He thought about his friends that he left behind at the job site, probably at home now, sleeping or watching TV, wasting their time. His mind kept wandering back to the night before at the pub. They needed money. They needed a new job. Not just a new construction job, but another "extracurricular" job. Frank had brought up doing a bigger job, and the guys had agreed that a bigger score would be nice. But what sort of job could they pull? What opportunities were out there that were good enough to bring in a big score, but doable for them? Then he remembered Matthew and his field trip.

Frank remembered Matthew talking about his trip to a rare book library, the reason he wasn't at work yesterday. Matthew had said there was a Shakespeare book there that was worth six million dollars. Or at least, it was last time it was sold. Who even knows when that was, Frank wondered to himself. *That thing's gotta have appreciated in value by now*, he thought, *maybe it's like ten million*. He grinned at the idea, trying to remember if Matthew had said anything about whether or not there was any security, or something like that? He had been a few beers deep by then so his memory was a little spotty. He had sobered up by the end of the night, but some parts were not that clear.

Now, what was that place called, Frank asked himself. He sat on the couch, unable to recall the name. He swayed forward, shifting his weight to help gain momentum, and launched himself up off the couch. He walked into the kitchen where his wife's laptop sat on the counter. He hit the power button and waited for the computer to power up. He stood at the counter, tapping his fingers on the surface impatiently. After several minutes, he opened up the web browser, and googled "rare books library Toronto." His search resulted in 2.6 million results. Fuck, he thought. He looked at the first result. "Home| Thomas Fisher Rare Book Library – University of Toronto." The name rang a bell. "That's it!" Frank said aloud to the empty kitchen. "Finally some luck on my side." He slammed his palm on the counter in celebration and clicked the link. He skimmed the introduction and went straight to the "about us – location" page. There was an address and driving directions. "Perfect," Frank said aloud again. He got a pad and pen from the phone table in the corner of the room and jotted down the address and directions. He changed out of his work clothes, stepped into his shoes, grabbed his keys, and left the house.

❖

Forty-five minutes after Frank left his house, he pulled into a parking lot just down the street from the Thomas Fisher Rare Book Library. He got out and began to walk up St. George Street. The day had gotten hotter since he left the house. His new set of clothes was beginning to reach the same damp state as his work clothes from that morning. He felt sweat on his brow and wiped it away. He felt beads trickle down his back and soak into his shirt, which stuck to his skin. The cool breeze from the morning was gone. Occasionally, a breath of cool air would brush against him, but any steady breeze was blocked by the buildings and houses of the downtown core of Toronto. The sun was high in the sky, and there were no clouds to be seen. *This place better be air conditioned*, he thought to himself as he pulled at his shirt, trying to cool himself. He reached into the front pocket of his jeans. "Ah shit," he said. He patted his other pockets looking for his pack of smokes. He stopped in his tracks, turned around, and walked back to his van. He grabbed his smokes, pulled one out, and lit it as he leaned back against the side of his vehicle. He puffed on the smoke, and pushed himself off the van onto his feet. The alarm beeped as he pressed the button on his keys and began to walk towards the library again.

He walked up St. George, passing groups of students milling about on the streets. Some stood around talking while others rushed off to their next class. These few blocks of the street were devoted to the residences and academic buildings of the University of Toronto's downtown campus. The library itself was part of the campus that stretched along St. George and across several other city blocks.

Frank walked up the street looking around at the stressed

students, fumbling through textbooks and notebooks. You don't know stress yet, Frank said in his head. Up ahead, at the next intersection, he saw his destination. He tossed down his cigarette, just the butt end now, and stomped out the ash. He looked up at the building in front of him. The building reached into the sky before him. It stretched up past the trees and beyond the lights lining the streets. A concrete tower centred the shorter building behind it. Six storeys up, flat grey face. A new tier stretched out from the rectangle reaching forward, like a lid for the top of the rectangular box. Apparently, the building was designed to look like a goose. Frank wasn't sure what sort of acid trip the architect was on when he decided that, but he had a feeling it was a bad one.

Frank crossed the street and turned to walk up the eighty or so steps to the entrance. They were small steps, short and wide, and odd for Frank to manoeuvre. They rose very little and stretched back far. There were way more steps than there should have been, he thought.

Frank reached the top of the stairs and, knowing he couldn't smoke inside, pulled out another cigarette and lit it up. He leaned against the rail on the top step. The entrance to the library was a giant glass and steel wall. It was a hallway connecting the tower to the larger building behind it, almost like a giant vestibule.

He puffed away, watching several students walking in and out of the library. He tried to look inconspicuous as he stood there, casually checking out the girls that walked by. He nodded to himself as he spied ones that he would have no problem sleeping with. He finished up his cigarette, stamped it out, and walked through the entrance to the library.

The floor was carpeted and softened the footsteps of the visitors. Frank stepped across the floor, looking left and right for a help desk. To the left was a wall with a revolving door that led to the tower. Above the door was a sign that read, "Thomas Fisher Rare Book Library." *I thought I was already there...here...there?* Frank thought, confusion clouding his mind as he cocked an eyebrow at the sign. He walked to the door, pushed on the handle, and walked through. The dull murmur of the students in the hall disappeared as he reached the other side. It was deathly quiet inside. He was definitely in a library. In front of him was a reception desk, turnstiles on either side. Frank was now in the tower he had seen as he walked up the street. There was a main floor that reached through the centre of the tower from one side to the other. He looked past the reception desk into the library. The walls were lined with books. Every floor.

Small, narrow paths circled the walls and ladders leaned against the shelves on every floor. The lighting was dim. Incandescent bulbs shone onto the floor but away from the shelves. The atmosphere of the room and the whole building itself, ironically, screamed "library." Frank walked up to reception desk. The woman behind, sitting down, looked up at him.

"Hello there," said Frank, resting his arm on the counter and leaning down towards her.

"How can I help you?" she said dryly. She was in her mid-fifties, probably closer to her sixties. Frank wondered if, in the entire history of libraries, there had been a librarian who was under the age of fifty. She had thick glasses hanging from a chain around her neck. Her grey cardigan was draped over her shoulders, covering the flower-print dress shirt underneath. She looked up with tired eyes, crow's feet reaching out from the corners of her eyes. Time had not been kind to her. Her hair was brown with streaks of grey, curly and fell down onto her shoulders. *Destined for the lonely, solitary work of a librarian*, he thought.

"Uh, yes. My son goes to York University," lied Frank, "and he was telling me about this Shakespeare book you guys have here. A folio? I think he called it."

"Ah yes, sir. We do have the Shakespeare folio here," she replied to him.

"Oh, great!" Frank said with enthusiasm. "Is there any chance I could see it? Look at it?"

"Well, sir, due to its being such a rare book, and having the value it does, we rarely, if ever, bring it out for singular visitors," she explained. Frank looked at her, cocking an eyebrow. "We generally have it on display when there is an exhibit running in the library. We had one a few months ago. I'm not sure when, or if, there will be another anytime soon."

"Oh, damn," said Frank. He slunk his shoulders in disappointment. He stared at the counter for a few seconds and then said, "but, my son came with his class the other day and said he saw it."

"Oh. Well, in some cases we do bring books out for class visits and things like that, but those are rare in themselves," she explained while twirling her pen in her hand. Frank noticed she had quite nimble fingers for an older woman.

"So, I guess you guys you have it back in the vault or something, right? With, like, armed guards and laser alarms?" Frank joked.

"Actually it is just put away on the shelves here," she said as she waved her right arm, gesturing to the walls of the library behind her. Frank looked past her, up the walls, across, and back down to the floor. Frank reckoned that there had to be a few hundred thousand books on the shelves.

"So, I guess that you guys know where to find stuff and it's all organized, eh? Wouldn't want to lose Mr. Shakespeare," Frank said smiling. She smiled back at him, a hollow smile, polite but strictly a customer service smile that she had practised and used for years. They looked at each other, eyes locked and both smiling fake smiles to keep the atmosphere friendly.

"If you would like more information about the folio itself, visit our website."

"Oh, is there more info on there?" asked Frank.

"Yes, quite a bit. I think we have some pictures there too," she said. Frank raised his eyebrows with interest.

"That would be good," he said softly.

"One of our librarians is a bit more qualified to tell you about the folio, but I'm not sure he's here today."

"Oh? Really? Does he work often?"

"He's usually here, and is usually the last one to leave he loves it here so much. James Vanderwood is his name."

"Oh, okay," Frank said, making a mental note of the name. "Maybe he'll be here tomorrow?"

"He should be. Definitely in the evening. He's not that hard to miss. Almost always in a sweater vest. Grey hair, white goatee. He can definitely give you some insight into the folio."

"That would be great!" Frank said, feigning enthusiasm. He took mental note of the description, vague as it was, and stuck it to the name he already had for the man. "Well, I'll try to run into him another day," Frank said with a smile. She smiled back and again the two locked their gazes in a moment of awkward silence.

"All right, well, ummm, thanks for your help," said Frank, breaking the staring contest and looking around the room casually. He looked in corners, above the desk and at the wall across from the doors. Hmmm, he thought, no cameras. He sighed and began to turn away.

"Thank you for visiting the Fisher Library, have a nice day," said the librarian, all while looking down at her desk. As far as she was concerned, their conversation ended several minutes before and she was eager to return to her crossword hidden under a book on the desk in front of her. Frank walked towards the door, and turned to smile back and wave at the librarian as she offered her goodbye. His smile faded as he saw that she wasn't paying any attention to him. He looked around the room again, checking corners, and looking for any other doors to the main floor. There was an elevator to the left of the front desk and a small office to the right. The door was half ajar and Frank could see inside. Nothing special, he thought. He could see a desk, chair, and a couple of shelves with books and papers strewn across both.

Frank walked to the revolving door and pushed his way through. He left the solitary silence of the library and entered the hallway of dull murmurs and footsteps. He took a moment to look around the hallway as he patted his pockets and found his cigarettes. He walked to the door leading outside, waited as two students walked in. Frank reached past them with his arm to hold the door open as it began to close behind them. Frank gave them a cold stare as they passed him, upset that they didn't give him the courtesy of holding the door for him after he let them through first. He pushed the door open, walked outside and took a deep breath.

Frank cleared his head and body of the smell of the library as he inhaled several deep breaths of the hot polluted city air. He then popped a cigarette into his mouth, lit it, and sucked back the smoke. He returned to the ledge he'd leaned against when he first arrived at the library and smoked his cigarette, watching the people walking on the street below. He wiped his forehead with four fingers and shook the excess drops of sweat off before wiping the rest of the dampness on his thigh.

Frank looked up to the sky, sighed and exhaled the last puff of smoke from his lungs stamping out the butt on the ground. He walked down the steps and crossed to street to the street meat vendor set up on the sidewalk.

"Hey! What can I get for you, my friend?" asked the man operating the cart. He had a big belly that pushed out the apron he wore. His black T-shirt clung to his thick arms, and out of the top sprouted a large head. Stubble covered his two chins and his scraggly black hair stuck to his forehead. He turned and rotated the few sausages he had cooking over the grill with a pair of tongs, and looked over them at Frank, waiting for an answer.

"Hot dog, buddy. And a pop. Coke. Thanks."

"Hot dog and a Coke," repeated the cook. Frank dug into his pocket looking for change. He watched the cook as he separated one tube steak from the rest. He turned it with the tongs and sliced diagonally across it with the knife in his other hand.

Frank pulled out a handful of change and fingered

through it finding a loonie, a toonie, and two quarters. He pocketed the rest of the change and reached over the cart towards the cook.

"Three fifty," said the cook as he saw the money in Frank's hand. Frank paid the man and stood back from the cart, looking out over the street turning his head away from the plume of smoke coming off the grill. He turned back as the cook was placing the hot dog into the bun that had been toasting. The cook reached over the cart, handing Frank the hot dog. "Here you go, my friend. And," said the man pausing as he reached down into the fridge portion of the cart and took out a red can. "Your Coke," he finished, handing Frank the can.

"Thanks, buddy," said Frank. He grabbed the ketchup bottle sitting on the top of the cart and squeezed a red stripe onto the hot dog. He placed the ketchup bottle back and took the mustard. He squeezed a yellow line alongside the red one and put the bottle back on the cart. "Have a good one," Frank said as he turned and walked down the street.

Frank finished the hot dog in several large bites and snapped open the can of Coke to wash it down. He hiccoughed as he took the can away from his lips after downing half of its contents. The can was wet with as much perspiration as Frank. The water dripped down the side of the can and down onto the pavement where it dried up in seconds. Frank finished the Coke and tossed the can into the garbage just as he reached his destination, the parking lot. He took out his keys, opened up his van, and climbed in. He started up the vehicle, turned the air condition on full, and sat, waiting for the air to reach its maximum coolness.

Frank sat in his van and closed his eyes as he felt the

cool air hit his face and arms. His moist skin combined with the cool air to create an extreme cooling effect. Frank smiled as he felt the heat melt away. He then reached into his pocket, took out his phone, and dialled Steve's number. He waited as the phone rang three times.

"Yeah?" Steve said, answering the phone.

"It's Frank."

"Yeah, what's up?"

"Call the other two, meet at the pub tomorrow night. I think I got a job for us."

Seven

The Foxhound was pretty empty for a Friday night. Frank walked in and let the big, heavy door swing shut behind him. He took a quick survey of the pub and walked to the back of the room, towards the booth tucked away in the back. He had told Steve to tell Kev and Jack to meet at the Foxhound for nine o'clock. Frank got there fifteen minutes early, to try to make sure he got the back corner booth he wanted. He knew the discussion that was going to take place and wanted it to be off in a corner, out of the way. He had thought about having the meeting at a random place, perhaps a deserted parking lot, but decided on the pub.

Frank walked over to the booth he spied when he walked in and eased himself into the bench seat. He shuffled to the inside of the booth and emptied his pockets of bulk: phone, keys, and smokes. He placed them on the table and flipped open his phone to check the time and see if he had missed any texts from anyone. He hadn't. He sighed as Becky walked over to him.

"Hey, big guy," she said as she reached the edge of the table. She placed a few coasters on the table as she talked. "Can't be just you tonight, can it? A little solitary beer time?"

"Nah," Frank said putting on a smile for her. "Just got here a bit early. Rest of the boys should be here soon. Could probably start off with a pitcher of Coors? Thanks."

"No problem!" Becky said with enthusiasm. Frank shot her a smile and turned back to his phone as it buzzed with a new text. He flipped it open and checked the message.

"Where r u?" read the text from Jack. Frank raised himself from the seat and turned to look towards the front door. Jack stood there, hands in his pockets, looking around. Frank nodded towards him as he caught his eye and Jack returned the gesture with the flick of his head.

"Back corner, eh? You hiding from someone?" Jack said with a chuckle.

"Just sit down," said Frank. Just as Jack plopped into the bench seat, the cushion exhaling with a whoosh as it accepted his weight, Becky returned to the table with a stack of four glasses and a pitcher full of the beer Frank ordered.

"Hello Jack," Becky said with a flirty tone.

"Oh, hey Becky. How's, uh, how's the night going?" he asked, as he glanced up at her and then quickly away, still feeling embarrassed from their encounter the other night.

"It's good, thanks," she said. "I'll come back when the other two get here?" she asked both Jack and Frank.

"Yeah, sure," said Jack. Frank nodded, his concentration on the beer he was pouring into a glass. He slid the full glass over the table to Jack and then poured his own.

Jack looked up from the table, his eyes wandering around the room, half watching the people and half looking for Becky, to admire her figure. His eyes passed over the front doorway and he saw Steve walk in followed by Kev. Jack threw them a wave as he saw them scanning the room as he had when he arrived. Steve and Kev walked over to the table, sat down and grabbed a glass each to fill.

"How's it goin' fellas?" asked Steve as he tilted the

glass towards his lips, taking a sip.

Frank closed his phone. "Good. Well, not bad," he said.

"Yeah, not bad," said Jack.

Kev looked up, and then directly back down at his beer as he saw Becky approaching. He hadn't looked above her neckline as she approached and felt his cheeks redden, thinking that she had caught him staring at her.

"Now the gang's all here!" Becky said as she got to the table, opening her arms wide towards them. "So we have the first pitcher done," she said reaching over the table, picking up the empty pitcher. "Another one? Any food tonight?"

The four guys looked across the table at each other and nodded in agreement for the second pitcher.

"Yeah, second pitcher," said Steve.

"Okay," said Becky.

"And I'll get a banquet burger," said Jack.

"Yep, burger for Jack. Anyone else?"

"Umm," said Kev, "fries and gravy."

"Nothin' for me," said Frank.

"Yeah, same, nothing for me," said Steve.

"Alrighty boys," said Becky. She turned on her heel and walked away, the four guys unable to resist watching her as she bounced across the floor.

Frank shook himself back to reality and said, "Okay boys... to business."

"Yeah," said Kev, "I'm surprised you already found a job. Who'd you talk to? Derek at KR?" asked Kev, referring to a company they worked for previously.

"No, no," said Frank. "It's..." he said pausing and lowering his voice. "A side job."

"Ah, gotya," said Steve.

"Still," said Kev, "something so fast?"

"Yeah. Well, the option presented itself a couple of days ago. I've done a bit of research into it, and it's doable. It's a big payout."

"Yeah?" asked Jack. "Well, we did say we were okay doing a bigger job.

"Exactly," agreed Frank.

"Okay, so what is it?" Steve asked. The group leaned forward towards Frank as he leaned over the table.

"Well," Frank started, "remember what Matthew was talkin' about the day we were here?"

"That chick he was trying to go after?" said Jack with a confused face.

"No, you idiot. Always thinkin' with your dick," said Frank.

"That book thing?" Steve asked.

"Exactly," confirmed Frank.

"Wait," said Jack, "you're talking about that Shakespeare play book?"

"Folio. It's called a folio," said Kev.

"Okay, like that matters, it's a book," said Jack.

"It's different," said Kev. "It matters to some people."

"Okay, doesn't matter. The name isn't the point," said Frank.

"So what?" said Steve in a hushed tone. "You want to," his eyes darted around the room, "steal it?"

"Yeah," said Frank matter-of-factly.

"How many beers did you have before we got here?" said Jack with a chuckle.

"No, it's not that stupid," said Frank. "It's six million

bucks! And I went there, and—"

"What? You went there? To that library? You went there to see it?" asked Steve.

"Yeah, yeah. Just, let me explain," said Frank. Jack leaned back in his seat, as did Steve.

Kev sat forward, his elbows resting on the table.

"I went there Wednesday, after I left the site," Frank began, but he paused when he noticed Becky approaching out of the corner of his eye. He leaned back from the table as she arrived. She had two plates of food balanced on her left hand and forearm, and a fresh pitcher in her right hand.

"Here you go, guys," she said placing the pitcher on the table. She took the fries with her now free hand and placed them on the table in front of Kev. She reached over the table and placed the plate with Jack's burger into his outstretched hands. "Be careful, Jacky, the plate's hot. Wouldn't want you to burn yourself," she said in a teasing tone, smirking and giggling. Jack closed his eyes and gritted his teeth. His cheeks flushed. "Thanks," he said dryly.

"Anything else, boys?" she asked. Jack, Frank, and Steve shook their heads.

"No, this is good," Kev said as he stuffed a few gravy-covered fries into his mouth. Becky smiled and walked away.

"Right, anyway," Frank said, drawing everyone's attention back to his story. He took a sip of beer and continued. "So, I went there after work the other day. Figured it was worth checking out at least to see how much of the kid's story was true, and it's pretty much exactly as he said. I talked to a librarian there, and there is no security or vault. The room where the books are is pretty big, but all the books are just on the shelves. You just have to know where they are specifically. There is a specialist or something that works there. The reception girl says he stays late most of the time and is the last guy there."

"Okay, hold on," said Kev, trying to grasp the task that was being set up before them.

"So, there's no security, no guards, no vault to keep the books? Nothing?"

"Nothing."

"Cameras?"

"Nope, I checked that too. I didn't see anything. Even if there are, we are prepared for that." Kev nodded. "Yeah, true enough."

"So yeah, I worked up a bit of a plan. And we can do it. We have everything we need."

"Okay, what do we do?" asked Steve.

"Well, simple enough, we go when it's just the one guy there alone at night, get the book, and leave."

"Well that's simple all right," Steve said with a chuckle.

"Yeah, well there is a bit more to it. Like, we gotta get the guy to tell us where the book is, so we might have to threaten him or something. Everyone reacts to the barrel of a gun. And I have a backup if he's stubborn."

"Okay, before that backup plan, they'll report that book missing and then be looking for it. How do we get rid of it when it's so hot?" asked Kev. "And who's going to buy it?"

"Black market antiquities and shit," said Steve.

"Exactly," said Frank. "I already talked to Jones, and he said he knows a guy who deals in that stuff."

"Jones? We're back on good terms with him? After Jack fucked his girl?" asked Kev with a laugh.

"I didn't know," said Jack, defending himself.

"Well, good enough terms to do business," said Frank. "And don't worry about it being hot," said Frank, looking at Kev, "nobody's gonna know it's gone until we've already sold it."

"How?"

"We're gonna burn the place."

"Serious?" asked Steve.

"Yeah. We take our book and then we just torch the place. If anything, they'll think it was lost in the fire. Won't matter. It will take them like a week or something to figure out what we got, if they figure out anything at all."

"Hmm," said Kev. "Seems like a good enough plan." He leaned back in his seat, crossing his arms, his mind racing at the possibilities, as well as all the possible flaws. Steve nodded in agreement and took a big sip from his glass. Frank drained the remainder of his beer and put the glass back on the table.

Jack looked blankly at the rest of his burger which sat in front of him, half-eaten. His mind worked slowly but eventually caught up to the rest of the group. "Yeah, this can work," he said.

"Okay, well back to that contingency you mentioned, Frank, if the guy is stubborn."

"That's the second part. I went back there yesterday, to see this guy and scout him out like any other job. He seems pretty easy. I don't think there will be a problem. He looks like you would expect a library specialist to look like," he said with a laugh. "Old professor-like with a beard and stuff. But yeah, I followed him when he left, and he lives kinda far from the library. He has a house in a quiet little neighbourhood like thirty minutes away. North part of the city. He has a wife and a kid, but the kid is long gone out of the house, all grown up."

"How do you know that?" Kev asked.

"Through conversation. But don't worry, it was just an accidental conversation. I saw him walking out and bumped into him while pretending to be on the phone yelling at my son. I dropped the phone, and I think it's fucked now, but he was all apologetic, and I just vented about my son and asked him if he knew what it was like and all that crap. Just made up a bunch of shit and he was nice enough to tell me what was waiting for him at home."

"Okay, so what about it?" asked Jack.

"Well," said Kev, "if I may?" Frank gestured him to go ahead. "I'm guessing we send one of us to the house to use the wife as a hostage. A little influence for this guy if he tries to be a hero." Frank nodded, as Kev had read his mind.

"Hostage!" Jack said in a harsh whisper. "You sure we can do that?"

"Yeah, it's easy! You just get her in the house, point a gun just in case, and then it's all good. Don't worry, you're probably not going to be that guy," explained Frank.

"Good," said Jack with a mouthful of burger. He washed it down with a sip from his glass. "Good, I don't want to do that."

"Pussy," said Kev. Jack shot him look that told him to fuck off.

"What do you think, guys?" asked Frank. "Everyone in?" He looked around the table.

They all exchanged glances before answering.

"I'm in," said Steve.

"Yep," said Kev.

"All right," said Jack.

"Good," said Frank.

"Let's make some money," said Steve with a smile.

"All right, boys," said Frank. "I'll finish up my preparations tonight and tomorrow, and I'll call you to go over everything again on Sunday. We can probably do it Monday."

"So soon?" asked Steve.

"Why not? Why wait?" Frank replied.

"Yeah, okay," said Steve.

"I'll talk to Jones, see about his connection, try to get a buyer lined up, and at least set the stage for a buy," said Frank.

"Sounds good," said Kev.

The four sat at the table for an hour longer, finishing up their drinks and chatting about this and that. Becky came by a few more times, once again igniting the argument of whether she was flirting with someone at the table in particular or just working for tips. Jack maintained that she was doing it for him, which he knew she was, but kept his sex with her a secret. Just as she wanted it. He didn't want to risk losing her over bragging to his friends, though he was tempted almost every day.

People kept wandering into the pub throughout the night, and by the time the foursome was ready to leave, the pub was "packed tighter than Becky's outfit" Steve had commented. They made their way through the crowd after paying and saying goodbye to their favourite waitress.

They walked out of the pub into the night, split up as they had the last time they were there, and made their ways back home.

Eight.

Kev opened the door of his car, got in, and reached across to unlock the passenger door for Steve who entered the vehicle and closed the door. Kev started up the car, which hummed to life after an initial groan, and both men buckled in for the ride.

"What do you think?" asked Steve.

"Of the heist?"

"Yeah."

"Seems good. I think we can pull it off. Doesn't seem to be any real danger or anything," said Kev.

"Yeah, that's what I thought," said Steve.

"I've gone over Frank's plan in my head. It seems like it will be simple enough. I just can't believe there is no security. There has to be cameras if there are no actual security guards."

"He said he didn't see any."

"Yeah, but maybe he missed them."

"Maybe, but it doesn't matter, does it? The way we go into these jobs, the only thing people can tell is height and build. And none of us is one-of-a-kind. There are other people that look like us. And we have our faces covered. It's all generic stuff we cover ourselves in. Like, it's nothing that's special order. It's all available at Walmart or Home Depot. Anyone could get it."

"Yeah, you're right. It just seems too good to be true, and when you can say that, it is."

"I dunno, man, sometimes things go your way. Karma, you know?"

"Yeah, maybe. So, what, you think this job is the universe making amends for us fucking up that doorway?"

Steve laughed. "Maybe!"

The roads were busy with traffic and the drive to Steve's place took longer than usual. People wandered the streets in their clubbing gear, hopping between clubs, going to new ones, leaving them, stumbling. It was the nightlife of a busy city. Cars beeped as taxis dodged in and out of lanes.

Kev pulled up to Steve's apartment and let him out. Steve went to the front door and waved as Kev pulled away, back into the street and the nighttime traffic.

Steve walked into his apartment, changed into his sleepwear, and plopped down in his chair. He turned on the TV and flicked around for something to watch. He stopped on *Lock, Stock and Two Smoking Barrels*, deciding it was appropriately themed considering the main conversation of the night. The movie was halfway through when he stumbled upon it. He watched the rest and then turned in for the night.

Kev gave a nod as he saw Steve wave from the front door of the apartment. He pulled away from the curb, back into the street and the traffic. He cranked up the radio and lost himself in the songs that blared through the speakers. Twenty minutes later he arrived at his apartment. He pulled into the underground parking, down to the second level, and parked in his usual spot. He was happy to see nobody had taken it.

Kev entered his apartment, locked the door behind him,

and went directly to his gaming chair. He turned on the TV and the Xbox and settled in for a night of gaming. He knew he had no reason to get up early the next day and smiled, knowing he could stay up through the night with no consequence the next day.

❖

Jack got into his Civic, started the car, and turned up the radio. He had nowhere to be and began to drive home. He had physically healed from his experience with Becky a few nights ago, but her comments tonight had opened the mental wound. He didn't like that she kept making fun of him for it, but he didn't want to let it get to him. He was failing. It was getting to him. He was ready to wait for her. Ready to wait for her to finish her shift and then confront her about it, express his anger and tell her that she was upsetting him, but he didn't think it was necessary. *Maybe if we were in a relationship*, he thought, *but we're not*. She'll just see it as me being weak or emotional. She won't really care. She has no obligation to care. And I guess she's just having fun. He thought about it for the beginning of the drive home, and he soon forgave her for her comments, allowing his mind to wander to the proposition Frank had made earlier.

He knew he had suggested the idea of taking on a bigger job the other night, but he wasn't sure about parts of this new job. He was fine with the stealing of merchandise, but he never felt comfortable hurting anyone. When Steve had smacked the jeweller over the head in their last visit, Jack had cringed in his mind. He was happy with the plan as long as he wasn't the one holding the wife as a hostage.

Jack went over Frank's plan. It made sense. He hadn't planned any of their side jobs. He was not comfortable making the plans, and could never think of everything. When his friends brought up issues he hadn't thought of, he kept quiet at the table, wondering to himself how they came up with those situations. Jack knew he wasn't the smartest of the bunch, and so he took his place as a follower rather than a leader.

Jack made his way home at a steady pace. He sat in some of the same nighttime traffic that Steve and Kev had driven through. The drive went by quickly as his mind was busy thinking about Becky and the heist. He yawned, pulling into the tenant parking lot adjacent to his building. He got out of his car, making sure his tenant parking card was properly displayed on the dashboard. His Civic beeped as he locked the car remotely, slightly echoing in the quiet night. Jack took out his phone and walked, thinking about messaging Becky, but deciding against it. He was still upset over her comments, but he felt he would be over it by the morning.

Becky had affected him unlike any other girl he had spent nights with. Ironically, it was the fact that she didn't want a relationship with him that made him want a relationship with her. Jack knew it was stupid, but he couldn't help his feelings.

Jack rode the elevator up to his floor, walked down the hallway, and unlocked his door.

He entered his apartment, flicked on the lights, and locked the door behind him. He undressed in his bedroom, tossing his dirty clothes into a pile in the corner of the room, making a mental note that he needed to do laundry soon and climbed into bed.

Jack lay on his back, the sheets pulled up to his chest, and stared at the ceiling. He felt his eyelids grow heavy. He fidgeted and stretched out across the bed as he felt a wave of exhaustion wash over him and take him off to sleep.

❖

Frank got into his van and sat, fiddling with his phone. "Fuck sakes," he exclaimed out loud to himself as he smacked the phone in his palm. The screen blinked to life and then flickered out. "Ahh, dammit!" he cried out, slamming his palm against the steering wheel. He tossed the phone onto the passenger seat and started the van.

Frank gripped the steering wheel with both hands and closed his eyes. He needed to calm down. He breathed in deeply and exhaled slowly. He repeated this several times and then opened his eyes. He looked over at the phone on the passenger seat, frowned, and turned his attention to driving. His body performed the physical tasks, but his mind stayed on the subject of the proposed heist.

He felt satisfied with himself. The meeting had gone as he had planned. The boys were on board. He had thought out the plan carefully, how to present it to the group and how to gain their confidence.

Frank was smart and experienced. He had been pulling side jobs for much longer than any of the other guys and was confident in his abilities to pull them off. He was the one who brought the most jobs to the table, and more often than not planned and took the lead on them. In some cases, the situation required one of the other guys to take the lead, but Frank laid out the plan so carefully and so expertly that each guy had no problem following it. During his explanation, Kev had raised all the issues that had filled Frank's mind when he first decided that stealing the folio was a possibility. They thought alike, and Frank knew that Kev was smart. He was the one to double-check Frank's proposals and ideas, and anyone else's when it came to these side jobs. Together, their plans were flawless, and their teamwork was the reason that the group had never been caught.

Frank made his way home, thinking about what he had to do the next day to prepare for the job. Two days was not a lot of notice to give the guys and to prepare, but he knew they could do it. If it didn't look like they could pull it off, they could delay it another day or so. It wasn't like they had any other work to take up their time. He knew that he had to call Jones and try to set up a buyer.

Tony Jones ran a pawn shop downtown, but he also dealt with black market goods. He had connections all over the city, province, country, and in the States. Frank wasn't completely sure if he had connections overseas, but he assumed that he probably did. Frank had met Jones several years earlier when Frank had been doing jobs on his own and developed a good rapport with him. Frank would bring in goods; Jones would give him a good payout and then sell the items himself at a profit. In rare cases, and this folio would be one of those cases, Jones would call his connections and set up buyers for the more specific products that Frank would bring in. Kev had brought up the incident with Jack and Jones' girl, and although it was still a fresh wound for Jones, Frank knew that money healed all of Jones' wounds. Jones used bills as bandages, and any amount could cover up a scratch. So, Frank was confident that there would be no problem. He had already called Jones earlier that day to let him know there was a job in the works, and that he would need a buyer in black market antiquities. Jones said he would make some calls and see what he could do. Frank was to call him and follow up the next day.

With the buyer situation put to the side, and somewhat taken care of, Frank knew the next thing was to make sure they had all the materials they would need. They usually had everything they needed already from their construction work, including their disguises. Keeping things very anonymous was a strong part of not getting caught.

Frank pulled into his driveway and parked. He opened the side door and took a quick inventory of the items he had in the van that could be used. He then checked the garage and, satisfied with what he saw, closed up both his van and the garage, and headed into the house. He was going over the heist in his head when his wife interrupted his thoughts.

"Frank," she said, "I don't know how you can go out all the time. You just leave us here all alone!"

"Jessica, honey," he said with a tired voice, "I had to go out to meet with the guys to discuss work."

"Oh. Work, huh. Right."

"Yes. We have a new job coming up, and we need to assign tasks and stuff," he said. Frank never told his wife about his side jobs. At least, he never said what their true nature was. He always told her that he had picked up some side work from "a guy on the site who needs an extra labourer for a night job." She bought his explanations as these side jobs would bring in money. She was happy as long as he was providing for his family.

"Oh, okay. How is work going?" she asked, walking into the kitchen. Frank followed her and sat down across from her at the table. She began to leaf through the weekly fliers, circling grocery items on sale or items that they needed.

"Work is going along. Same 'ol stuff," Frank explained to her. He sighed and watched her. He admired her beauty and how she kept herself in shape having given birth to two children. She was gaining weight as she gained years, but she still looked damn good to him.

"This new job should bring in some good money," he said.

"Oh?" Jessica asked, raising her head as the idea of more money caught her attention.

"How much?"

"Not too sure, but should be a good amount."

"Oh," she said, returning her focus to the fliers spread on the table's surface.

"Well, don't you worry about it," Frank said, groaning as he rose from the chair. He pressed on the table with both hands, pushing himself up. "I'm tired though. I'm heading to bed. You coming?"

"Yeah, just after I finish going through these. Need to go get groceries tomorrow morning," she explained, never turning her gaze from the papers.

"Okay. Girls are asleep?"

"Of course."

Frank nodded and walked out of the kitchen, leaving his wife to her task. He walked up the stairs and gingerly opened the door to his daughters' bedroom. He kissed each girl on the forehead, wished them goodnight, whispered "I love you" in each girl's ear, and went to his bedroom. He undressed and climbed into bed. He lay there awake for several minutes, planning the next day before he nodded off to sleep.

Nine

Kev woke up at 10:07 a.m. to the sound of his phone, notifying him of a text message. He rolled over to the edge of his bed, reached up to his bedside table, and grabbed his phone. He opened his eyes groggily, unlocked the screen, and selected the new text message.

Pick you up at 6 tonight. Stakeout

Kev selected the message and deleted it, erasing any evidence of a planned stakeout. Kev was careful, the most careful of the group, and the self-proclaimed smartest of the group. Kev reached over the table and slid the phone onto the edge. He closed his eyes and began to roll over, pulling the sheets back up to his chin. The phone teetered on the edge of the table before tipping off and falling to the carpeted floor with a dull thud. Kev groaned, pulled the sheets up over his head, and fell back asleep.

Frank pulled up to the curb in front of Kev's building just as the clock on the dashboard blinked to six p.m. Kev was waiting out front, leaning on the grey brick wall. He pushed himself off when he saw the white van pull up and walked over to meet it. The door unlocked with a click as Frank hit the button on his door. Kev climbed in and buckled himself in.

"How's your day going, Frank?" asked Kev.

"All right. Went out, got some supplies, talked to Jones.

Things look good," replied Frank.

"Yeah? Does he have someone already? Or a contact?"

"Well, sort of. Said he knows someone who deals in the antiquities market. He contacted him, and has him looking for 'interested parties,' as he called them."

"I guess that's progress."

"It's better than what we can do on our own."

"True enough," said Kev. "So when you asked him, you didn't say what the item was, did you?"

"'Course not. Just said I might be acquiring an item that historical types might be interested in."

"Historical types, eh?" Kev said with a laugh.

"Yeah, I figured that covered it."

The sky was clear and the air was cooling down. Frank drove towards the library. The traffic was light, but beginning to pick up. There was a Leafs game starting in an hour at the Air Canada Centre, and that usually brought in extra tourists. They saw Leafs jerseys scattered among the pedestrians heading to bars and in the direction of the big sports arena.

They turned on to St. George St. and drove south. As they drove past the library, Frank pointed it out to Kev. "There it is. It's in that tower part of the building."

"That looks pretty big," observed Kev.

"Nah, it's not really. Once you're inside it looks smaller. It is tall though."

Kev looked out the window and scanned the building, turning his head as they passed it.

"Okay, so there is a parking lot around the back of the building that is for the library and the rest of the building. Last time I was here, I saw the librarian guy, our mark, go to his car there. Red Dodge," explained Frank.

They pulled into the lot, which was fairly small, about thirty or so spots and rather empty. There were several cars parked, including a red Dodge.

"That it?" asked Kev, as he spotted the car.

Frank craned his neck to the side to see it. "Yeah. That's his."

"This guy works on a Saturday?"

"Well, it's a library. It's open all the time, I guess."

Frank backed the van into a spot in the far corner of the lot. The front faced the building, and the red Dodge parked near the front of the lot. Frank turned off the engine. He unbuckled his seat belt, and Kev did the same. They settled in to wait.

Kev took out his phone and checked the time. "Six-fifty," he said. "So, when does this guy finish?"

"The last time he was done around eight thirty. I figure he might finish earlier 'cause it's Saturday."

"All right, well, turn on the radio or something. Leafs game is starting soon," Kev said tucking his phone back into his pocket.

Frank turned the key, so the radio clicked to life and pressed his AM preset 2. Joe Bowen's voice came through the speakers, introducing the starting lineup for the Leafs, and talking about the team's last few results.

"Who they playin' tonight?" Frank asked.

"Rangers," Kev answered. He wiggled in his seat, trying to get comfortable. "They're in a bit of a slump, should be a win tonight. But you know how it goes, you take those struggling teams too lightly, and then you lose."

"Yeah. Gotta' play like it's against first place all the

time."

The two sat in the van, listening to the game and keeping their eyes on the entrance of the building and the red car diagonally across from them. A couple of people had come out of the building since Frank and Kev arrived. They disappeared into the darkening evening, leaving behind Frank's white van, the red Dodge, and one other silver Buick.

Time passed as Frank and Kev listened to the game. The first period was winding down, and the clock on the dash read 7:40. Kev was looking at his phone and Frank was looking out the window. They were both relaxed, beginning to feel groggy as night fell upon the city.

Frank's eyes were glazing over as he looked across the lot to the dull grey exterior of the building. The glass doors shimmered as they opened, light bouncing off them and reflecting away. Frank saw the light distortion out of the corner of his eye and almost disregarded it, but shook himself awake as he recognized the person walking out. He sat upright, reached across, and tapped Kev's shoulder several times saying, "That's him. There he is. That's the guy."

Kev's eyes opened wide and then narrowed as he squinted for clarity, looking out into the darkness. He watched a man with a white beard, in a long brown trench coat, carrying a briefcase, walk from the entrance towards the red Dodge that sat quietly in the parking lot. He pointed his hand out, and the Dodge beeped and blinked. The man walked to the trunk, opened it, put his briefcase inside, and closed it. He walked around the side of the car and climbed into the front seat. The car hummed to life.

"Definitely the guy we're looking for. Unless he's a very casual thief," Kev said with a chuckle.

The Dodge pulled out of the parking space and turned out onto the street. Frank turned on the van, it thrummed into life, and he pulled out after the Dodge.

"Do you remember where he lives? Or do we have to *follow* follow him?" asked Kev.

"I mostly remember. We can sit back a bit. Don't need to be too close," said Frank calmly.

"All right, cool," said Kev.

They drove, following the red Dodge carefully. They kept back enough to not be noticed, but at times, Frank pulled out in front, knowing the next bit of the route and then slowed down to let the car pass. By going out in front, staying farther behind, and not following too closely, Frank blended in with the rest of the traffic on the street.

As they reached the librarian's neighbourhood, Frank sat back a little further in the thinning traffic. They delayed their turns just slightly and casually drove along behind their target. They watched the red Dodge pull into the driveway of a little bungalow, and continued past, pulling over to the curb a little farther down the street.

The street was neat; the residents took care of their properties. Lights lit up rooms inside some of the houses, showing signs of life, but the street and sidewalk remained empty except for a few parked cars.

Frank and Kev watched, in the reflections of the van's mirrors, the librarian get out of his car. He retrieved his briefcase from the trunk and walked into the house.

"Okay, so here it is," said Frank.

"All right," said Kev.

"You can remember where to go?"

"Yeah."

"All right. So, it's pretty simple. House is small. Street is empty, and hopefully will be on the night, too. It seems like a quiet street anyway."

"Shouldn't be a problem. Once I get in, it'll be simple and routine. So what should I do once she is under control?"

"I think we should be arriving at the library around the same time as you arrive here. I'll send you a text to say we are ready to go. Once you respond, we'll go in. Should take like half an hour or something to get it done. If we need to, we'll call you and you can put her on the phone, they talk for like twenty or thirty seconds and then hang up. I'll send a text when we have the book. If we don't need to call you, I'll just send the text that we have the book."

"Okay, sounds like a plan," said Kev.

"Yeah. So while you're here—"

"Keep a low profile," Kev said finishing Frank's sentence. "I know. Nothing big, don't draw attention. Shouldn't be a problem."

"Yeah. Keep yourself hidden. Make sure she can't identify you."

"No shit, Frank."

"Yeah," said Frank. "Now, if it comes to it, even though it shouldn't, can you pull the trigger?"

"I know you guys kind of mock me a bit, think I'm a nerd with the video games, but don't worry. I can get shit done. More so than Jack, anyway," said Kev.

"Okay, good. And yeah, what was that the other night? He's usually tougher, or at least plays tougher," Frank said, reaching forward and brushing some settling dust off the steering wheel.

"Just make sure he doesn't chicken out and fuck the whole thing up while you're there."

"Yeah, don't worry, I can handle him," said Frank with assurance.

Frank started up the van. "All right, let's get out of here," he said. Kev nodded, and they pulled away down the street, leaving the house in the rearview mirror. Kev watched the house in the side mirror as they pulled away, watching it get smaller and smaller until it disappeared around a corner.

Ten

As the sun slunk into hiding for the night, two cars left the parking lot they had been sitting in for the last half hour and headed out for their destinations. The sky was clouded. It had threatened to rain all day, but it held off. The air remained hot and sticky as it had been through the weekend, with the threat of a thunderstorm lingering in the atmosphere.

Kev drove towards the suburban neighbourhood he and Frank visited on the weekend. He had made mental notes as to where he had to go, and had a couple of street names on his phone along with the house number. The drive was smooth, traffic was thinning as people got home and stayed home, fearing the skies would open and drench the world underneath.

Kev was just looking at his phone to see the street name and house number when it vibrated and rang in his hand, catching him off guard. He twitched at the surprise of the call and juggled the phone for a few seconds before he answered it.

"Yeah?" Kev spoke into the phone.

"Where are you? We just pulled up," said Jack on the other end.

"You're there? Okay. I'm just pulling onto the street. Couple minutes before I'm in."

"Okay. Call when you're set up."

"Okay," Kev said. He ended the call with the press of a button, and the line went dead with a click. He opened the note on his phone that included the address of the house: 187 was the house number. He was already on the street, and he looked out the window to see how far along he was. It was getting darker, and only a few houses had the outside lights on, lighting the house numbers. 158. 156. *Okay,* Kev thought to himself, *it's on the other side.* He kept a slow speed and carried on down the street, looking out the passenger side of his car. 167. 169. The houses counted up as he drove along. He looked ahead and saw his destination. He recognized the garage door.

He recognized the little bungalow and the white garage door. It had crescent windows along the top row of panels of the door. The house was dark brown and red. Kev drove a little farther past the house and pulled over to the curb.

He looked out the front window of the car and up the street. There was a woman walking her dog, or at least it looked like a woman. Kev saw a dark shape holding a thin line attached to a dog. You couldn't always tell by a person's walk, but he thought, woman. He saw nobody else.

Kev turned in his seat to look behind him down the street. He saw two headlights of a car pull onto the street and head in his direction. He sunk into his seat, watching the lights in the side mirror. They grew larger as it approached, and lit up the interior of his car as it drove past. The red brake lights lit up Kev's face, and he reached up to scratch his head and cover his face from the lights. The car continued down the street and made a left onto another street. Kev sat back up in his seat looking around the street again. It was deserted. Devoid of life. Cars were parked in driveways and against the curb. Several houses had front lights on, or lights on in a room or two, but curtains were closed, and blinds were drawn. Satisfied that there were no people out on the street, Kev reached down into the passenger footwell and pulled up a duffle bag. He unzipped it and spread the bag open.

Kev was already dressed in his black track pants and hoodie. He took out the small jar of black face-paint, unscrewed the top, and dipped two fingers into the cool liquid. He reached up with his other hand and angled the rear-view mirror, so he saw his face. He rubbed his fingers over his face, applying the black paint to his cheeks, under his eyes, and his forehead. He turned his face in the mirror as he covered more and more of his skin with the paint. He rubbed the remainder of the paint from his fingers on the knee of his pants and rubbed the material to dry the paint. He fanned his face and double-checked his work in the mirror. His eyes, cheeks, and forehead were covered. He was satisfied with his work. He screwed the lid back on the jar and placed it back in the duffle bag. He reached in and pulled out the sunglasses and dust mask. He put the mask over his nose and mouth, pulling the elastic strings over his head and settled the mask on his face. He pressed the metal bridge on the mask that sat on his nose, pinching so the mask held its place. He picked up the sunglasses, wiped the lenses clean with the front of his sweater and placed them over his eyes. He looked in the mirror. He was now a race-neutral human being. No noticeable identifying features. Dark under the mask and glasses. He pulled the hood of his sweatshirt up over his head, casting further darker shadows over his face.

He smiled under the mask as he looked at himself, but no reaction was noticeable in his reflection. He was a shadow.

Kev looked around the street again and then looked in the bag for his gun. He pushed it aside as he remembered the gloves. They sat, scrunched in the bottom of the bag. He pulled them out. White latex gloves. His nose twitched as he smelled the latex. Kev was never fond of the smell and was always eager to peel off the gloves and wash his hands clean of the scent. He pulled on the gloves, wriggling his hand so his fingers reached the tips. He pulled the cuff of the glove over his wrist and released it with a snap. He wiggled his fingers and clasped his hands together. He felt hot and could feel his hands begin to sweat inside the gloves. He sighed heavily, reached into the bag, and pulled out the gun that lay within.

He held the grip and turned the gun over in his hand. He pulled the slide back, and slid it forward. He flicked the safety off, then back on. He released the clip, and slid it back in. He rubbed the barrel of the pistol, sliding two fingers along the length of the metal, feeling the cool steel through the latex. His fingers ran along the barrel until he reached the silencer; the new addition to his gun.

Frank had suggested that they get silencers for this job, especially for Kev. The quiet neighbourhood should remain quiet, even if Kev was forced to pull the trigger. It made perfect sense in his head and he let Frank take care of getting the silencers. When they met in the parking lot earlier that evening, before departing to separate destinations, Kev had screwed on the silencer and tested the new weight of the gun in his hand.

He felt the weight of the gun now. The weight of the

mission ahead of them, ahead of him. He wasn't used to it. None of them were. They hadn't done anything this big before, nor this risky. They had never needed to fire their guns. They only ever brandished them in the sight of their targets, and that had always been enough, but sitting in his car, gripping his pistol and feeling the front of it dip down under the weight, he felt that they would be pulling triggers tonight.

He reached into the bag and pulled out a roll of silver duct tape and put it into the front pocket of his hoodie. He zipped up the bag and tossed it back to the floor of the car.

Kev sat in the car for several minutes, staring down at the gun in his hand. He slapped the barrel in the palm of his right hand, holding the grip with his left. He balanced the gun in his hand, making sure he was used to the new weight. He ran through the plan in his head. He looked in the mirror at the blank face that stared back at him.

"Okay, Kev," he said out loud to himself. "Let's do this shit. Keep it clean." He pocketed his keys, opened the door, and stepped out of his car. The gun was hidden from sight, tucked into his waistband with the shirt pulled over the top. He jogged quickly to the sidewalk, looking around for anyone he might see, but the street was still empty. The dark sky loomed above. Kev moved quickly up the front path of the house and stepped onto the porch. He turned his back to the door and rang the doorbell. Immediately, Kev bent down on one knee, and clutched his stomach with one hand and reached up bracing himself on the wall with the other. The wooden front door opened, and a middle-aged woman stood there looking out. She saw him kneeling, looking hurt, and heard him moaning.

"Oh my God!" she exclaimed as she opened the storm door. Kev moaned and grunted louder as he heard her.

"Unnffghh, help…" he muttered with a raspy voice.

"Oh my God, what happened?" she said, kneeling down over him, propping the door open with her body. "Can you move? Can you get up?"

Kev nodded and slowly, his face still turned away from her, pushed himself up off his knee into a low crouch, bending forward, still holding his stomach.

"Come inside," the woman said, moving aside and holding the door.

Kev entered through the front door in a controlled stumble. *Man, some people are too nice and too trusting*, he thought to himself. He walked into the hallway, and the woman followed in after him. The storm door closed behind her on its spring, and she pushed the big wooden door closed behind her. She came up behind him, rested an arm across his back, and reached to hold his other hand and guide him into the house.

"What hap—" she started, but before she could finish, Kev stood straight up, pulling the gun from his waistband as he stretched up. He spun to face her and pressed the gun into her stomach.

The masked, hooded face stared out and the woman saw her own terror in the reflection of his glasses. She gasped, her mouth dropping open and staying open, eyes wide in shock.

"All right, Miss," said Kev in a forced gruff voice, "let's just take it easy and do this calmly. Do what I say and everything will be fine."

"Are, are you going to rob me? Are you going to…" she

paused, shuddering at the thought, "k-k-kill me?" She stared down at the gun pressed into her belly. She could feel the cold metal through the light sweater she was wearing. The cold, blank face looked back at her.

"Not if you cooperate. It's easy. Let's just go to the kitchen first," said Kev in his forced voice, but calmly.

"Oh-O-Ohhkay," she replied nervously. She turned as he pulled the gun away from her. She began to walk to the kitchen slowly, her body stiff, arms hanging rigidly by her side. She entered the kitchen and turned to face the masked man.

"Now," said Kev as he reached into his front pocket with his free hand to retrieve the duct tape. He kept the gun pointed towards the woman. "Pull out a chair and sit down," he instructed her. She nodded quickly and reached for the nearest chair. She gripped it and pulled it out. It scraped across the tiled floor. She let go and sat down on the chair.

"Good," said Kev. He walked over to her and handed her the duct tape. "Tear off a piece and put it over your mouth." She fiddled with the tape and complied. When she had pressed the piece over her lips, she looked up at him. "Good, now begin to wrap your hand," he said. She looked up at him with a puzzled face but began to pick at the seam of the duct tape. Once she got it started, she pulled the tape off the roll and stuck the end to her wrist. She began to wrap it around her wrist. Kev interrupted.

"Good," he said taking the roll from her hand. Kev tucked the gun back into his waistband and pulled both her hands around the back of the chair. He held her shaking hands together and grabbed the dangling roll of tape, slid his hand inside the roll, careful to avoid the sticky side of the tape, and wrapped her hands together. When he was satisfied that her hands were not coming undone, he pressed on the smooth side of the tape with one hand, pinching it against her skin. He grabbed the roll with his other hand and snapped it to the side, tearing the tape. He smoothed the loose end of tape against the rest of her hands and put the tape back in his pocket.

She looked up at him, through reddening eyes. They were moist with tears that were beginning to form. Kev rolled his eyes behind his sunglasses, "You're doing great. This will all be over soon," he said.

Kev walked to the other side of the room and took out his phone and called Jack. It rang once before Jack answered.

"Yeah," said Jack.

"I'm in. Set up. Good to go. You guys ready?"

"Yeah. Just suiting up. Then we're in."

"I'll wait for your next call."

"Good," Jack said. And with that, the phone went dead with a click as Jack hung up. Kev placed the phone back in his pocket and leaned against the kitchen counter. He put the gun down and picked up a magazine that lay on the counter beside him. He began leafing through the latest issue of *Maclean's* and checked the clock on the wall opposite him. 8:20.

❖

Frank drove. Steve sat in the passenger seat, and Jack had climbed into the back and sat on the dirty, tool-covered floor of Frank's van. He looked between the two front seats at the digital display of the dashboard clock. 7:45 it read. "Almost there?" Jack asked as he fidgeted in the back, looking through the duffle bag of supplies they had brought.

"Just up ahead," said Frank. "Call Kev. He should be almost there."

Jack pulled out his phone and pressed to call Kev.

"Yeah?" Kev said as he answered.

"Where are you? We just pulled up," said Jack.

"You're there? Okay. I'm just pulling onto the street. Couple minutes before I'm in," Kev explained.

"Okay. Call when you're set up."

"Okay," said Kev. The call ended and placing his phone into his pocket, Jack said, "He was just pulling up to the house. He'll call when he's in and set up."

"All right, cool," said Steve. Frank pulled up to the curb and parked. He chose a spot between streetlights, where it was a little darker so as not to be too obvious.

"Jack, put out the cones and road work sign," said Frank.

"Got it," said Jack. He slid open the side door and climbed out. He reached back in to grab the stack of orange and white pylons. He put one about two feet in front of each corner of the van. He went back to the side door, climbed in on his knees and retrieved the roadwork sign: a triangle sign, red stripe border and a depiction of a man shovelling a pile of dirt in the centre. He climbed back out, carrying the sign and stood the sign in one of the pylons. He got back in the van and slid the door closed behind him.

"That's set up," he said.

"Good," said Frank. He sat back in his seat looking out onto the street, checking the mirrors and looking around. Steve was doing the same.

"Quite a few people out there," said Steve.

"Yeah, don't worry. Nobody pays any attention to construction workers," said Frank casually.

People were scattered along the sidewalks. They walked alone or in small groups. Some carried school bags, others had grocery and shopping bags. Some girls walked with big purses and bags while others walked barely carrying anything.

"I don't get why those girls have those huge bags," said Frank.

"That's 'cause you're too old Frank. You don't get the young girls," said Jack.

"Oh, I guess you do eh, Jack?" replied Frank.

"Of course I *get* the girls," Jack said with a wink. Frank just frowned and shook his head. Steve laughed.

"Well, maybe they're carrying important stuff," said Steve. "Maybe they're on their way to their heist," he said with a chuckle. "You could fit a couple of Uzis in those bags," he said.

"Fuck Uzis," exclaimed Frank, "You could fit a couple of AKs in there. And grenades!"

"So, what, they're secret soldiers?" asked Jack.

"Well, would you suspect it?" Frank asked.

"Guess not," said Jack. "But there's a lot of girls walkin' around with big guns, if you know what I mean," he said laughing. He gestured with his hands as though he was holding a pair of large breasts. The other two laughed.

"Fuckin' A!" said Steve. "Look! There's a couple of bazookas right there!" Steve shouted pointing out the window at a very overweight woman walking down the street.

"Whoah!" said Frank and he snorted out a laugh.

"Damn, those are huge!" Jack said laughing.

"All right, all right," said Frank. "Calm down," he said chuckling. "Better start getting ready. Kev'll be callin' soon."

Jack fished around in his duffle bag, searching for the little jar of black facepaint.

He found it, unscrewed the lid, and offered it to the two sitting in the front seat. They each, in turn, dipped two fingers in the paint and began to apply it to their faces. Jack followed suit. When they were all satisfied with the application, Jack screwed the lid back on and put the jar back in the bag. He got out three dust masks, handed one to Steve and the other to Frank who put them on, and then put his own on. He settled it onto his face and started to pull out the sunglasses when his phone buzzed with an incoming call. It was Kev.

"Yeah," said Jack.

"I'm in. Set up. Good to go. You guys ready?" said Kev.

"Yeah. Just suiting up. Then we're in," said Jack.

"I'll wait for your next call."

"Good," Jack said and hung up. "Okay, he's all set up in there."

"Went smooth?" asked Steve.

"He didn't say otherwise," said Jack, "So yeah, I figure it was smooth."

"Good. A good start. Okay let's get this shit goin'," said Frank. Jack handed out the sunglasses and they put them on. They pulled their hoods over their heads. Jack reached into the bag and pulled out a small plastic bag of white latex gloves. He handed a pair to each and then took out two for himself. He tossed the little plastic bag back in the duffle bag and put his gloves on. The van briefly filled with the scent of latex.

Jack reached back into the bag and pulled out two guns. He looked them over and handed them to Frank and Steve. He then got a third out and zipped up the bag. Each masked, unidentifiable, featureless man checked his gun. They felt, as Kev had done, the increased weight of the guns with the newly added silencers.

"Hopefully we won't need to actually use these," said Jack. Steve and Frank exchanged a glance and went back to checking their gun: the barrels, silencers, slides, and clips. All seemed in good order.

"All right," said Frank, stretching back in his seat so he could tuck the gun into the waist of his pants. "Let's go."

Frank opened the driver's door and got out. He closed the door and walked around to the passenger side of the van and stepped up onto the sidewalk. Steve got out next, followed by Jack. They closed up the van and Frank locked it with a beep from his key chain. They walked towards the library that towered before them.

There were people on the street, but they carried on their way with their own business keeping their attention away from the threesome heading up the concrete steps. Construction workers were not a rarity in the city, and people paid no mind to them. Anyone who saw them assumed they were on their way to do some overnight refurbishing or renovations in the building. Nobody saw their faces, as they climbed the steps quickly and entered the building. The main lights were off and the hallway was dark. Frank led the way to the left and through the revolving door. Steve and Jack followed closely behind. There were several lights still on in the Fisher Rare Book Library. The lamp over the reception desk Frank had visited several days before lit up the desk and the floor around it. They moved towards the desk and around it. They went to the elevator and pressed the button. It lit up, and they heard the hum of the elevator as it rose to their floor.

The elevator itself was grinding to a halt, and the doors clunked open. They stepped in, crowding into the little cab as the door closed behind them. Frank looked at the panel of buttons in front of him. He pressed the button beside the number 1, which had a label taped under the button that read "Rare Book Library." The elevator hummed back into life and groaned down to the first floor. The doors opened and Jack dashed forward in a crouched run to the desk in the middle of the room. Their target sat behind the desk and looked up from his work as the doors to the elevator opened. He was startled by Jack's quick movement and began to stand up as he saw two other men exit the elevator. Jack slammed up against the desk on one knee. He reached into his waist and pulled out his gun. He rose up and towered over the desk, over the old man who was beginning to rise from his chair but was startled back into his seat by Jack's sudden appearance.

"James Vanderwood?" said Jack in a gruff voice. The librarian just stared back at him with wide eyes and an open mouth. Jack wiggled the gun at him. "Are you James Vanderwood?" he asked harshly.

"Y-y-yes," stuttered Vanderwood. He looked past the barrel of the gun pointed at him. He tried to see a face through the dust mask and sunglasses but saw nothing. He looked beyond this first man and saw the other two approaching, guns in hand. They all looked the same. Same clothes, same coverings, same guns. The only difference noticeable was each man's size.

"Wh-what do you want?" Vanderwood asked, struggling to get through the words as he tried to remain calm.

Nobody responded to him. Steve walked around the desk towards the librarian. He reached into the duffle bag Jack had carried in and pulled out the duct tape inside. He tossed the roll into Vanderwood's lap and said, "Start taping your hands together." Vanderwood looked up at him, then down at the tape in his lap. He turned the roll over in his hands and looked back up at the three men standing around him and the three shiny silver guns pointed at him. He decided to comply. He picked at the edge of the roll and got the tape started. He began to unroll it and stick it to his hand. As he did, he said, "Look, I dunno what you guys want but we don't have any money or anything here. We're a library. We just have books."

He felt a calm come over him as he began to talk about the library. His job meant the world to him. He loved his work. He loved to lose himself in the books, manuscripts, tablets, and scrolls that filled the shelves of the library. He felt calm and at peace when he was hunched over a desk, the light bathing the pages he was working on. His hands steadied as the calm washed over him.

Jack, Frank, and Steve watched and listened to the man, glancing at each other, smirking under their disguises. As Vanderwood began to struggle with the tape, Steve leaned over and grabbed the roll. He placed his gun on the desk and grabbed hold of Vanderwood's arms at the wrists. He wrapped the tape around several times, squeezing it tight so it stuck to the skin. He tugged at Vanderwood's wrists, tried prying them apart, testing the secureness of his tape job.

When he was satisfied that the tape wouldn't come undone, he ripped off the remainder of the roll. He put the tape back in the bag it had come from and picked up his gun.

Vanderwood was still talking, "I don't know what you expect to get out of this. I have no money. There is no money here. We have nothing that you would want. Just. . . Just let me go and leave, and I won't say anything. It'll be a misunderstanding and we can all go home. It's not like there are books here that are. . ." Vanderwood trailed off as he began to realize why these three men were here. "You can't be serious!" exclaimed Vanderwood. "You can't just take those! Those are of historical value! They are pieces of literature to be enjoyed! Works to be admired and—"

Steve cut him off with a smack to the head, "Oh, shut the fuck up!" He yelled, gritting his teeth as he smashed the butt of the gun into Vanderwood's temple. Vanderwood's head snapped back from the blow. A welt began to form where the gun made impact. Steve turned and stepped away from the desk, looking around the room, attempting to regain his calm. *I hate when they just ramble on and don't shut up*, he thought to himself, *like what do they think, we're just going to say "oh, okay, our bad, have a good one!" and just walk away? Fuck sakes.*

Frank and Jack exchanged a glance from under their sunglasses. Frank leaned over the desk towards Vanderwood. "All right, look," he said calmly, "we just want the Shakespeare folio. You're going to help us get it and then we will be on our way and so will you."

"The Shakespeare folio? Yeah, that would do it," Vanderwood muttered to himself. "I don't know what you plan on doing with it, but you can't sell it."

"Let us worry about what happens after we've got it," said Frank. "You just worry about getting it for us."

"What if I don't help you? What if I just refuse? Are you going to shoot me? Kill me right here?" Vanderwood asked. He had already been hit, but he wasn't sure if these guys were serious. He had to test them. It might have been stupid, but this library was his life, his home away from home. The books were his children and like hell was he going to let three strangers take away his children.

"Are we going to shoot you?" Steve butted in. "Well," he said walking towards Vanderood. He pushed the barrel of the gun into Vanderwood's forehead. "What do you think?"

"You don't have the guts for it," said Vanderwood, hoping to force them to lash out in anger again. Maybe he could get these guys to argue with each other somehow. Try to make them think one of them is unstable and turn them against each other. He had read stories about robbers and thieves in groups and he knew there was no honour among thieves and that they would turn on each other without a moment's notice.

"Shoot you?" said Frank. "No, we won't shoot you," he said. Jack reached into his pocket as he saw where Frank was going with the conversation. Steve pushed the gun hard into the skin of Vanderood's forehead, pushing his head back and then releasing the pressure and taking the gun away from his head. Vanderwood held back the smile he felt growing on his lips.

"But we will shoot someone else," Frank said. Vander-wood looked up at him puzzled. He looked quickly around the room and saw nobody else.

Jack walked around the desk, his phone in his hand and pressed the call button, Kev's number already inputted. He put the phone to his hear and heard one ring before Kev answered.

"Put her on," said Jack. He stood beside Vanderwood and pressed the phone against his ear. Vanderwood heard two voices on the other end. One male voice and one female voice he instantly recognized. He heard whimpers grow loudly as the phone was brought closer to her face. Vanderwood felt tears begin to form in his eyes as he put the scene together.

"H-h-hello?" said the shaky voice of Karen Vanderwood.

"Oh god," whispered James Vanderwood into the phone.

"James?" she said.

"Honey, don't worry. We'll get through this," he said, stifling the tears and sobs he felt. She could not show the same restraint.

"James, he has a gun pointed at me. He—" Her voice was cut off at the sound of a smack and her cry of agony.

"Don't you touch her!" he screamed into the phone.

Jack snapped the phone away from Vanderwood's ear and ended the call. He walked back around to the other side of the desk. Vandewood sobbed as he thought of his wife being held at gunpoint.

"I think you understand the gravity of the situation now," said Frank. "We are serious. Do not try us. Do not test us. Do not be a hero. Just do what we say."

"Fuck you! You, you," Vanderwood struggled to find the words he wanted, "you sons of bitches!"

Steve leaned over and smashed his gun into Vanderwood's temple again. The skin broke and a trickle of blood ran down his forehead. Vanderwood grunted and moaned in pain. He stared up at Steve with hatred in his eyes, a fire burning inside, but the fire died down as Steve raised his gun again. Vanderwood cringed and Steve laughed. "Bastards," Vanderwood muttered under his breath.

"So," Frank said, "are you going to cooperate now?" Vanderwood nodded. "Good. Now, where is the folio?"

Eleven

Kev tucked his phone back into his pocket. "Shut up," he said. Karen sat on the chair in front of him, sobbing, her head hung down and tears dripping onto her lap. He grabbed her by the throat with his hand. "Shut the fuck up. Stop crying," he said angrily. He raised his hand as though to hit her again and she closed her eyes and flinched. He released her and walked back to the counter and the magazine that he was half way through. He looked at his phone as it vibrated with a text from Jack: "all good."

Karen sat in the chair whimpering softly. Kev watched her from across the room. He felt odd. He knew he had to be rough with her to make sure she complied. To make sure she didn't get any ideas of struggling against him. He knew she was old and he could manage her in a fight, but sometimes things turned out differently than you expected. He reflected on the video games he played and the movies he watched, remembering the twists and turns that happened in those stories. Some were predictable and some shocked. But he had enjoyed them all. He smirked as he remembered some of the more fun moments he had lived through his virtual adventures and smiled again as he realized he was living one now.

He shook himself back to the kitchen and the woman sobbing on the chair in front of him. Back to the gun in his hand, not the remote or game controller. This was real. He had the power to kill in his hand. A simple flex of the finger was all it took. Pull the trigger and the firing pin strikes the primer which ignites the powder, and the bullet screams out of the barrel like a bolt of lightning, searing through the air until it penetrates the target. The metal pierces the skin, breaking the bone of the skull. The bullet would tear up the matter inside as it passed through the skull. Instant kill.

Kev had done it so many times in his games, seen it so many times on TV shows, in movies, but the reality of killing someone was different. It would affect him. He slid two fingers over the top of the barrel, feeling the smooth cold metal on his skin. He pressed the gun against the back of Karen's head and felt a shiver travel down his spine. His arm hair pricked up as the anticipation of the kill took him over. Kev smirked. He liked the feeling of power he held over another person.

Kev was small, always was. He had been picked on in elementary school. It died down a bit in the later grades, but picked up again in high school. Kev turned to video games for an escape. He needed a place where he was in control. He got that through video games. He controlled the character on-screen. He wielded the power. He took down his enemies. He kept to himself through high school but was still picked on because he was a small nerd. Then he began to hit the gym. Kev felt he needed to get bigger, so he began to work out. He went to a small family-owned gym just a few blocks from his home. He tried to go when it wasn't busy, and because it was a small place, it never really was. Kev went a couple of times a week and never gained much bulk, but he built himself into a strong adult.

He was still small, but he was powerful, deceptively so. He was happy with the results of his hard work.

Kev stood in the kitchen. Looking at the gun pressed against the head of the woman he only met less than an hour ago. He thought back to his younger self. The powerless kid he used to be. Pictured all the bullies he had faced and run away from. Pictured all of them at the end of the barrel, not Karen. He clenched his open hand into a fist. Gripped the gun harder, pressing lightly on the trigger. He ground his teeth, pressing them hard into each other at the back of his mouth. His lips formed a straight line. No smirk now. Just the anger he felt from his youth. The rage burned behind his eyes. He knew what he had to do now. What Frank had meant the other day when they came to scout the house. Kev had been nervous at the thought. But he had centred himself, focused, and done what he had come here to do. But now, replacing the current situation with hatred from his past, replacing the woman in front of him with the skeletons from his closet, he felt calm. Angry but calm. Karen's sobs fell on deaf ears as he pulled the gun back. Karen's sobs halted as she felt the pressure leave. A tear trickled down her cheek and fell onto her leg.

Kev looked at the end of the barrel of his gun and the silencer. He looked around the room. He didn't see a kitchen, he saw school halls. The lockers he had been slammed into. The floor he had been pushed down to. He saw the faces of the bullies he faced…Bang.

Kev closed his eyes and opened them again. He was back in the kitchen. He looked in front of him and saw Karen's lifeless body slumped on the chair, a quarter of her head blasted off from the gunshot.

"Where is the folio?" Frank asked again. Vanderwood looked up at the huge man standing in front of him. He blinked as the trickle of blood from Jack's blow ran down into his eye. He blinked again to send the drop on its way, continuing down his cheek.

"Okay, okay," Vanderwood said. "Just, don't hurt my wife."

"She'll be fine as long as you don't screw with us," Steve said with a smirk. Frank shot him a quick glance and then turned back to Vanderwood. "So, where?"

"It's through there," Vanderwood said as he hooked his head backward, arcing it towards the door on the far wall behind him.

"Okay. Good," said Frank. He nodded to Jack. Jack flipped open his phone and sent Kev a text to say that the librarian was cooperating and that he could leave. Closing his phone, Jack focused back on Frank who was stepping behind Vanderwood. "Now," said Frank, "here is what we're going to do. My two partners are going to keep their guns pointed at you, and I am going to lift you out of the chair." As Frank talked, Steve and Jack raised their guns to point at Vanderwood. Frank grabbed Vanderwood under the right arm and lifted him up off the chair with ease, even giving Vanderwood air time.

Vanderwood landed and stood on shaking, unstable knees. He stood up and straightened himself. He tried not to look as terrified as he was. His mind kept wandering back to his wife. She was all alone at home. There was at least one more of these thugs there. He wondered if there were more, and what he or they might be doing to her. He blinked away a tear and felt the hardening blood on his face. These guys meant business, and it wasn't worth fighting back. He thought about what they had said. They said if he helped, they wouldn't harm him. But guys like them always said that, didn't they? And then they just kill the helper anyway, right? But they were hiding their identity so well, they couldn't be recognized, so maybe they were telling the truth. Usually, they had to kill you because you saw who they were. But that's not the case here. Vanderwood decided to go along with them, to save his wife and hopefully his life.

"Good. Now we walk to where the book is, and you get it down for us," said Frank as he pressed his gun into Vanderwood's back. Vanderwood furrowed his brow and raised his bound hands. "You can still reach. You just proved that," said Frank. Vanderwood's shoulders slunk down as he realized Frank was right. "Okay, let's go."

Vanderwood walked towards the back room. The door was closed, but his fingers were free, and he could turn the knob. It was awkward, but he did it without protest. Frank and Jack followed closely behind while Steve stayed at the desk with the duffle bags.

The room was dark and as Frank entered he looked on both sides of the door frame to find a switch. He flipped the switch on the left side with the tip of the silencer of his gun. The room lit up with the soft yellow glow of two lamps against the left wall, on either side of a desk. The room was full of small two-seater tables and several individual desks. The kind of desks you saw in elementary school. The ones where the chair was attached to the desk. Frank shuddered as he remembered his childhood. He was always a big kid and fitting into those desks was a tricky and humiliating task. He shoved Vanderwood with his gun to take out his frustration. Vanderwood looked back over his shoulder at Frank and continued to the large office desk between the lamps. Jack stopped at the entrance of the room and leaned up against the doorway with an air of casual grace. He was tired; he wanted this to be over so he could go home and sleep.

"It's just up there. That one," said Vanderwood, pointing at a large case on the third shelf on the back wall behind the desk.

"So, get it down," Jack said from the doorway. Vanderwood reached up and, using his fingertips, pulled the case off the shelf. It began to slide toward him and fell off the shelf into his arms. He caught it and walked it over to Frank. "Here," he said angrily. Frank turned the case over in his hands carefully and awkwardly, as he still held a gun with one hand. The case looked like a book and on the spine were the words *Shakespeare Plays* embossed in gold. "Okay, back outside," said Frank. Jack pushed himself away from the wall and waved his gun at Vanderwood who understood the command. He walked towards Jack, who stepped aside as he neared, out the door and back to the desk. Jack motioned for him to sit back in his chair and Vanderwood complied.

Frank exited the room carrying the folio in its case. He put it down on the desk just as Steve said, "Open it. Let's make sure it's the real thing and he ain't lyin' to us."

"Of course it's the real thing!" exclaimed Vanderwood. "Why would I lie when you have my wife?!" he shouted.

Jack pressed his gun into Vanderwood's temple and

whispered into his ear, "Lower your voice." He shoved Vanderwood's head with the gun and Vanderwood opened his mouth to say something else, but thought better of it. "Better," said Jack.

Frank placed his gun on the desk and picked up the folio. The case was dark brown and worn like old leather. It was hard and shaped like a book. It was essentially a shell, shaped like its contents to protect it. There was a horizontal seam in the middle of the case. Frank pressed his fingers into it to loosen the top. He lifted the top off to reveal the treasure inside. It was big. This was no small book. The folio was 13.125 inches tall, 8.375 inches wide and 3 inches thick. Frank pulled it out of the bottom half of the case carefully. Vanderwood watched, wincing as he watched the big brute handle such a valued item.

To say the folio was old would be an understatement. It was from 1623, but it didn't look it. It looked used, yes, but not as used as one would think. The cover was pasteboard bound with brown leather. The same dark brown as the case. Two water rings on the top third, overlapping like the MasterCard symbol. There were little dents, divots, and scratches scattered over the cover. Around the border of the cover was an intricately embossed gold pattern of swirls, loops, and dots. The corner was bent and worn, a sign of the abuse it had taken over the centuries. On the spine, *Shakespeare Plays* and *First Folio 1623* was embossed in gold.

Frank lifted the corner of the cover gently, as carefully as Vanderwood would have, but for different reasons. Where Vanderwood didn't want to wreck a piece of literary history, Frank didn't want to decrease its dollar value. The spine creaked as Frank opened it and he halted where he was.

"Careful," warned Steve. Frank looked up at him, breathed out, realizing he had been holding his breath without knowing he was. He lifted the cover slowly and looked at the inside of the folio.

The inside cover had six stickers, known as bookplates, arranged in a sort of cross shape. When someone took possession of the book, they put the bookplate on the inside cover as their mark. On the first page of the book, written in pencil in cursive hand was, "Purchased from Harvey Frost in May 1955 slf STC 22273." Lower on the page, "very first tall copy: 13 1/8" x 8 3/8" was written.

"Yeah," said Frank, "this is it." Frank, Jack, and Steve smiled under their masks, looking at each other, exchanging glances.

Frank closed the folio and placed it back into the bottom half of the case. He replaced the cover on top, sliding it down until it settled into place with a hushed *pffi* sound. He picked it up, walked it over to Steve, and put it into the empty duffle bag. He nodded to Steve and quietly said: "Get the gas."

Vanderwood strained to hear what Frank had said but was unable to decipher more than "get the. . ." He hadn't heard the final word. Steve walked to the elevator, pressed the button, and disappeared as the doors closed. Steve walked out of the elevator and jogged through the rotating door into the foyer. He hooked right, went outside, and jogged down to the van, still parked on the roadside. He unlocked the doors with the keys from his pocket and opened them up. He pulled out two big twenty-litre gas cans that they usually used for extra gas in case they needed it on the job site for machines. Steve pulled them out, put them on the street, and closed up the van. He picked up the two plastic containers, one in each hand, and walked back up the stairs at a quickened pace. He wanted to get back inside quickly, and the gas was pretty heavy. He walked back inside the foyer, through the revolving doors and pressed the elevator button. He waited as he heard the motor hum to life. *Weird,* he thought to himself, *it should already be up here. I didn't send it back down.*

Only two minutes after Steve disappeared into the elevator, it chimed, and the doors opened. Jack turned towards the elevator, "Fuck me, that was fast!"

The doors opened, but Steve wasn't standing there. Instead, Jack saw a short, fat, greasy janitor. The janitor's eyes widened as they moved from Frank to the bloodied Vanderwood, finally resting on Jack, who would be the last person he would see.

Jack acted quickly. He twirled towards the elevator doors, bringing his gun up to aim. He gripped it with both hands and squeezed the trigger once, twice. The shots fired and hit their target. The first hit the shoulder of the janitor, staggering and turning him. He began to stumble forward when the second bullet hit home, right in the chest. He dropped to the ground with a thud as blood began to pool under him.

"What the fuck!" exclaimed Jack. "Jesus, who the hell was that! What the hell was he doing here?!" He turned to Frank. "You said there wouldn't be anyone else here!"

"Fuck. I didn't think there would be a fucking janitor here! It's fuckin' Saturday! Nobody works Saturdays here except this guy," said Frank gesturing at Vanderwood.

"Oh my God!" shouted Vanderwood. "What, you, how

could you shoot him?! Is he dead? Oh my God! Oh my God!"

"Shut up!" shouted Frank. He leaned toward Vanderwood and smacked him on the back of the head. Then again across the jaw with a right hook. Vanderwood shook from the blow and blinked away the oncoming dizziness. He began to sob, tearing up. He knew the janitor, Wilson. He had talked to him a number of times briefly during his time at the library. Wilson was a quiet man who never did anything wrong to anyone.

"He didn't deserve to die!" shouted Vanderwood.

"I said shut up!" Frank said, raising his hand to strike another blow. He stopped as Vanderwood cringed and closed his mouth. Frank turned back to Jack. "Drag the body over here. This'll work." Jack looked at him with a puzzled face under his disguise. He went over to the body, crouched down and began to drag it by the arms.

The elevator came; Steve got in and hit the button for the lower floor. The doors opened to a scene he wasn't expecting. Jack was at the desk dragging a janitor across the floor leaving a large trail of blood back towards the elevator.

"What the fuck happened?" Steve asked as he stepped out of the elevator, making sure not to step into the blood. He walked over to the desk and put the gas containers on the ground.

"Well," said Jack, "I shot this guy."

"No, fucking shit. Who is he? Where did he come from?" asked Steve.

"Janitor. Upstairs somewhere," Jack replied.

"How the hell did we not see him?" Steve asked.

"I dunno," muttered Frank. "He must've been on another

floor or in some room."

"So, how did he get down here?" asked Steve.

"Well," said Jack, "the elevator. It binged, the doors opened, and I thought it was you. What a surprise to find this guy standing there. I reacted and shot him. Twice."

"Wait, wait," said Steve. "You heard the elevator, thought it was me, and pointed your gun at the doors?"

"Well I only pointed the gun when I saw this guy," explained Jack.

"I hope so, jeez," said Steve. "I guess we gotta get rid of him?"

"Yeah," said Jack, "but don't worry. He has a plan apparently," said Jack, nodding towards Frank who nodded.

❖❖

"Fuck." Kev looked at the mess, then looked at his gun. His knuckles were still white, and he was still gripping the gun with full force. The situation hit him like a punch to the stomach, knocking the air from his lungs. He took a deep breath and then began gasping for air. "Oh fuck, fuck, FUCK!" He yelled.

He reached into his pocket to grab his phone. He wanted to call Frank, ask him what he should do, but he knew he couldn't. They were probably in the middle of their part of the job. He slammed his phone back into his pocket. He thought back to the car ride, on the scouting drive to see the house, Frank had said to him, "Now, if it comes to it, even though it shouldn't, can you pull the trigger?" Kev had answered with confidence. He knew he could do it. He assured Frank it wasn't a problem. But it wasn't supposed to come to this. It didn't need to. He had read the text saying it was all fine. The librarian was going to cooperate. He didn't need to kill the woman.

He walked around to the front of the body. He looked at the mess of a face in front of him. "I'm, I'm sorry. I didn't mean to…" he trailed off. No point in apologizing to a corpse. He felt his hands quiver slightly, then, realizing this was not the time to panic, clenched his fists. *Right,* he told himself, *leave no trace and get the hell out.* He had his tracks covered. He had gloves on so there was no problem there. No fingerprints. He thought over the situation in his head. Were there kids? He couldn't remember. Was pretty sure there weren't. There was just the husband, the librarian. He wasn't going to make it home, at least that's what Frank had told him in the car ride back after they scouted the house.

"Don't worry about cleaning up the body if it comes down to it," Frank had said. "I'm gonna take care of this librarian guy, so he won't be coming home. He ain't gonna find her. There's nobody else, at least nobody else living there that is gonna come back to find the body. Maybe the neighbours after a week or something. All you gotta do is make sure that you don't leave any trace behind. Wear your gear like always, and if you gotta shoot her, you gotta find the bullet. No trace. Got it?"

Kev had agreed. He understood his next step. He tucked his gun back into his waistband and looked around the room. Bits of brain, blood, and bone were splattered over the table and the wall in front. He walked over behind the body, lowered himself a little so that he was looking right over the top of the body, looking through the section of her head that was missing. He looked straight ahead at the wall and saw a bigger, darker splotch on the wall: the bullet. Walking over to the counter, he carefully opened the top drawer to find the cutlery. He took a steak knife and went over to the wall. He poked at the splotch and cupped his hand underneath the hole, pried gently with the knife until the bullet plopped out of the wall and fell into his hand below. He kept the bullet in his hand along with the knife and left the kitchen. He walked to the front door and looking outside, saw nobody around. His hands were sweaty inside the gloves and trembling slightly as the realization of the mess he made dawned on him. He looked down to grab the doorknob and realized that his clothes had a spray of Karen on them. "Ah fuck," he muttered. He walked quickly to his car. When he reached the trunk, he opened it. He pulled off the mask, glasses and then his sweatshirt. His pants were clean, maybe some spatter, but nothing noticeable. *I'll toss 'em anyway later*, he thought to himself. He turned the shirt inside out and balled up the knife and bullet within. He closed the trunk, got in the front, started the car and drove off, looking in the rearview mirror at the house he was leaving behind.

Kev drove in silence. He was on high alert, looking for anything or anyone that might've seen him or would be following him, but he was clear. There hadn't been anyone on the street to see him leave the Vanderwoods' house. He needed to get rid of the evidence of his crime. He thought about how he could do it and where, and came to a decision. He pulled into the parking lot of a supermarket, parked near a sewer grate, and got out. The night was cool, but Kev found himself sweating. He wiped his brow with the back of his hand and rubbed the moisture off onto his pants. Kev took the sweater from the car, knelt down over the sewer and unrolled the shirt over the sewer. The bullet rolled out, clinked off the edge of the grate, and fell into the water below. The knife rattled on the grate but didn't fall. Kev looked around, saw nobody near, and stood up. He nudged the knife with his foot until it fell through and sunk to the bottom of the drain with a splash. Kev balled up the sweater and got back into his car, tossing the sweater into the passenger side footwell. He started the car up and drove on.

It was getting late. He hadn't heard anything from the other guys but hadn't thought about it until now. He had been so preoccupied with his tasks that he had nearly forgotten about the real reason this was all happening. He pulled his phone out of his pocket. No messages, no missed calls. Okay, they hadn't called, he hadn't missed anything. They were still working. He thought to himself about it. *Shouldn't they be done by now? Unless something went wrong with them too? Shit. Okay, don't worry. They can handle it. There are three of them, just one of you and you did your part, handled your mess. Just get rid of the shirt now.*

Kev kept driving until he came across a construction site. It was small, a renovation of some Tim Hortons or something, one of those little cafes. Kev reached into the back of his car, grabbed his hard hat that he kept there, and put it on. He grabbed a lighter from the glove box in the car, and the balled up shirt and walked over to the fence. There were people around, but they either walked right by without looking or looked once and looked away, paying no special attention to a construction worker at a construction site.

The fence was a temporary one, so it was easy to pop out the top clips and raise it up off the metal bases on the ground. Kev had done it hundreds of times at other sites, so he went through the action flawlessly, like he belonged there, once again, just blending into the construction site. Someone struggling with the fence would've drawn attention, but Kev did it smoothly.

He walked into the site, around to the other side away from the pedestrians. He threw the shirt onto the ground, bent down on his haunches, and flicked the lighter on. He placed it next to an edge of the shirt and let the flame catch on the fabric. The flame grew and spread over the shirt. Kev stood up and watched the flames engulf the garment. The smoke rose up. He watched the fabric turn to ash and felt the guilt of the killing drift away with the smoke.

Twelve

"So, you have a plan?" Steve asked Frank. "What's this plan?" he said. "We went with your plan to start. Nobody was supposed to die. You said you did all this shit, you scouted, and there was just this guy!" Steve said, his voice raising, hand stretched out pointing at Vanderwood, who was still slumped in his chair, head down, sobbing as tears trickled down his face.

Frank stood a few feet away from Vanderwood, but was still close enough that he wasn't going to miss. He was a decent shot. He had been hunting once with his dad when he was fifteen, and had taken down a deer on his second shot of the day. He hadn't gone again as his father passed away the next year from cancer, but Frank always cherished that memory of his father. He always felt that he made his father proud with that shot, and he wondered if his father would be proud of him now, but quickly scratched that thought and brought himself back to where he was. Standing several feet away from his next hunting target.

He didn't want to kill the librarian. But he knew he had to. He had seen Jack kill the janitor. They had to eliminate him. He had kept this back-up plan in the back of his mind from the beginning. He figured he would kill the guy anyway, whether they were going to get out clean or not, but now there was a better reason to shoot him than just to be safe. He knew Steve would protest. It was hard to argue for killing someone who could not identify them and who had done nothing wrong.

Frank raised his gun arm, pointed the gun at Vanderwood's head, and cocked it. Vanderwood heard the gun cock and raised his head toward the sound. He turned to see Frank standing to his left with the gun pointed directly at his head. Vanderwood's lips trembled, and the tears began to flow freely as he realized he wasn't going to make it out alive. He had cooperated for nothing. He should've known. They were going to kill him. Of course. Maybe they would've let him go. His logic earlier was sound, he couldn't identify them and he had helped them, but then the janitor showed up and ruined it. Now he was a witness to murder. His time was up.

"N-n-no, p-please don't. I won't say an-any-th-thing. I don't kn-know wh-who you are," Vanderwood mumbled between sobs, "I-I-I can't and-and won't say anything. Just, please, d-don't shoot me." He looked towards the elevator. He couldn't see the janitor's body as it was on the floor on the other side of the desk, but he could see the beginnings of the blood trail leading to it and the spatter on the wall. He prayed that if he was going to go, let it be quick and painless.

"We can't kill this guy!" Steve shouted at Frank as he saw him raise the gun. "Why? What for? He's not going to say shit!"

"He's seen too much," Frank said matter-of-factly. "We have to."

"He hasn't seen anything!" Steve protested. He felt like he was the only one of the three that had a conscience. He was okay with the idea of roughing someone up, but that wasn't permanent harm. He had talked to Jack about the possibility of killing before. They had been using guns for a while now but never needed to shoot. Jack had sided with him. He didn't want to kill anyone either, and felt sick thinking about it. But now he had shot the janitor and he didn't look affected at all! Was he lying before? Or did something just take over his mind, like a killer instinct? Steve wasn't sure, but he knew that he himself didn't have it. He didn't feel the same way about it all. He couldn't do it.

"I'm not standing here and let you kill him!" Steve yelled. He made a move toward Frank but saw Jack move and stopped in his tracks. Jack had turned toward Steve and raised his gun.

"What the fuck, man?" Steve shouted.

"Sorry man, but he's right," said Jack, nodding at Frank. "This guy's got to go too. I didn't want to shoot this guy," he said pointing at the janitor at his feet, "but it happened, and he saw me do it. I can't have him walking around. Liability."

"But you were against shooting people, man! You wanted to kill as much as I did, which is not at all! What happened? Did he convince you?" Steve said, pointing his gun at Frank.

"I didn't say shit," said Frank. "He's just a smart boy."

"Fuck off!" Steve yelled.

"He's right," Jack said. "He didn't say anything. Last night I was lying in bed and I couldn't sleep thinking about today. This job. It all went through my mind. The plan, the alternatives, the ending. It came to me," Jack said with a calm voice, "it has to happen this way. Even if the janitor didn't show up. We gotta eliminate him. He knows what we took. The reason you have that gas is to hide what we took."

Vanderwood looked between all three masked men. He saw the corner of a gas can sitting on the ground just around the front of the desk. "Wait," he said, "you can't be thinking of. . ." his voice trailed off as he pictured the library going up in flames. All the books and manuscripts saved over years all gone because of these thugs. "No! You can't! I wo—" but Vanderwood didn't finish his sentence. Frank stepped forward, pressed the gun against Vanderwood's temple, and pulled the trigger. Vanderwood's head snapped sideways and then fell forward, blood running out of the wound onto the rest of his body and onto the floor.

"Fuck!" yelled Steve.

Frank bent down and began to unwrap the tape from Vanderwood's hands.

"What the fuck are you doing?" yelled Steve.

"My plan," Frank said. He undid the tape and balled it up, being careful so it didn't stick to his gloves and rip them. He tossed the ball of tape aside. He lifted Vanderwood out of the chair, stood him up as best he could, and shoved him sideways, in the direction the gunshot would've sent him. Then he placed his gun in Vanderwood's hand, wrapping the three fingers and thumb around the handle, one finger over the trigger.

"Drag the janitor over there, back towards the elevator. Position him how he was when he fell," said Frank. Jack tucked his gun in his waistband and bent down over the janitor's body. He dragged the corpse back to where he had been shot, just outside the elevator. Steve stood in awe, his mouth open behind his mask. "Okay. What the fuck, man?

What is this plan?"

"Murder suicide," Frank said.

"Huh?" Steve furrowed his brow, confused. "How the hell does that work?"

"Well, say this Vanderwood guy was pissed off at the world, hated his life, and just wanted to torch the place and kill himself. Whoops, the janitor showed up, so he shoots him, then sets the place alight and kills himself. There you go, cops are happy if they find this place and put that story together, it makes sense and no worries. Okay? Now start pouring that gas everywhere," Frank ordered.

"Are you fucking nuts? How the hell are they going to make up that story? You think they can come up with that?" Steve said.

"Seems easy enough," Jack said as he walked past Steve to the gas cans. He picked one up and unscrewed the lid. He walked to the far side of the wall and began to shake out the gas inside the can.

"Holy shit," said Steve in disbelief. He picked up the second can and walked over to Frank. As he passed it to him, he said, "This better work or I swear I'll take you down."

"It'll work," said Frank confidently.

Steve began to pour the gas over Vanderwood's body, then the janitor's, and began to spread the gas over the walls and floors. Frank walked round the front of the desk, picked up the two duffle bags and slung one over each shoulder. Jack emptied his can and tossed it to the floor. He went to the desk, grabbed a handful of paper, and rolled and scrunched it into a torch shape. He reached into his pocket and pulled out a lighter. Frank called the elevator.

"We ready?" Frank said. Jack nodded. Steve tossed his empty gas can and jogged to the elevator and stepped inside.

"Flame on!" yelled Jack. He smirked as he sparked the lighter, lit his makeshift torch and tossed it at the feet of the gas covered Vanderwood. Jack turned and ran to the elevator stepping in just as the doors began to close. The three turned and watched the flames creep up the body of the librarian as the door closed. Jack pulled out his phone and sent a message to Kev: *Done. Meet up.*

They rode the elevator to the main floor. The sound of the fire alarm started just as the doors opened.

"Let's go, let's go!" yelled Frank. They jogged out the revolving door, through the foyer and outside. They hurried down the steps to the van. Steve grabbed the pylons he had put out when they arrived and climbed into the van. Frank started it up and they drove away. Jack looked out the side window at the building. It looked no different than when they arrived. Not for much longer.

Frank drove carefully but quickly. The steering wheel felt slippery under his hands. The gloves were hot, they didn't breath and he was sweating. He was beginning to calm down the further they drove.

There was a scheduled meet with Kev. He was to meet them in the parking lot of a Rona. Jack had sent Kev the "job complete" text as they left the library, but he hadn't received any response yet. Maybe Kev just hadn't seen the text yet, or just didn't reply. Maybe something had gone wrong? Frank had exchanged a worried glance with Jack when they were five minutes away from the library and hadn't gotten a response from Kev yet.

"You think there was a problem?" Jack asked.

"Doubt it," Steve said. "He didn't have to do anything, right? The librarian cooperated so he didn't have to do anything to the wife. 'Course, we didn't have to do anything to the librarian…" Steve trailed off. He understood now why they had to shoot the librarian, but he wasn't happy about it. It still didn't sit well with him. It wasn't part of the plan he knew. It wasn't part of the cover their tracks and leave no evidence plan. Steve sat in the back of the van with crossed arms, glaring through his sunglasses out into the night.

"He's probably just bein' lazy, or his phone's on quiet or somethin'," Frank said, stretching his hands out over the steering wheel.

"Can we take this shit off now?" Jack asked, tugging at his mask.

Frank only now realized he was still wearing the mask, glasses, and hoodie pulled up over his head. "Oh, right. Yeah. We're far away enough. Steve, bag." Frank reached up to his face with one hand and pulled off his mask, glasses, and pulled back the hoodie. He reached back and dropped the items into the garbage bag Steve held out. Frank pulled off the gloves one at a time and balled them up into a sweaty latex mess. He flipped the ball back without looking and it dropped right into the bag. Jack did the same with his gear, and Steve followed last, tying up the bag when he had put the last of his gear inside.

Frank reached up and wiped the top of his head. He was wet with sweat. He dried his hand on his pant leg and relaxed back into his seat.

Jack's phone vibrated in his hand. "Oh, look who's finally responding," he said dryly. He flipped open his phone, saw Kev's text, and relayed it to the rest of the van. "He's on his way there," said Jack.

Frank looked in his mirrors. A white Dodge Charger was slipping in and out of the two lanes, between cars and getting closer. It wasn't moving too fast, but Frank noticed it amongst the dark night. It stood out because of the light bar on the roof.

"Fuck," Frank muttered under his breath.

"What?" Jack and Steve said simultaneously, both looking out the van for whatever Frank must've seen.

"Behind. Cop," Frank said grimly.

"Ah, I'm sure it's nothing," Jack said, seeing the police cruiser in the side mirror. It was still pretty far back and it was quiet. No noise. No lights.

Steve turned around to look out the back of the van. "Yeah," said Steve, agreeing with Jack, "probably just going to Timmy's for a cruller," he finished with a laugh.

"Still," said Frank, his voice unsteady with unease.

Frank drove on, keeping the speedometer needle hovering just above or just below the fifty kilometre speed limit. The cruiser stayed behind them. It was no longer weaving through the traffic, but sitting back as if it was waiting for something. Waiting for them, it seemed.

Frank looked down from the rear-view mirror, out the window to the side mirror. His vision was split three ways. Rear-view mirror, side mirror, and forward through the windshield. His head was positioned forward but his eyes darted from each location furiously and often.

"Oh, fuck off," Frank said angrily as he saw the lights on the cruiser turn on. "Fuck sakes!"

"No way," said Steve, looking out the back and seeing the cruiser roof light up with red and blue.

"Gun it, Frank," said Jack.

"Are you nuts?" Steve yelled at Jack. Frank sped up. The sirens blasted. The rise and fall of the *woooooohhhh woooooooohh* of the sirens shot a chill up Steve's spine and sent goosebumps up his arms and neck.

Frank watched the cruiser pick up speed and pull forward, the cars in the left lane slowing to let it pass. The cruiser stayed in the right lane, pulling up behind their white van.

"Fuck this," said Frank. He sped up, pulling away from the cruiser, and away from cars in the other lane. The cruiser stayed right with them, matching their speed.

"Just fucking boot it, Frank!" yelled Jack. "Get us the fuck outta here!"

"Frank, just pull over, there's no way they'll get us for the library. How could anyone know it was us? Maybe your tail light is out or something."

"Fuck that!" yelled Jack. "We got the fuckin' book and guns in here. We can't risk this shit. Maybe someone saw us leave, and then saw the flames or something. If we jet they can't do shit. We can lose them. Foot down, Frank!"

The cruiser pulled out beside their van. It sped up and within seconds the side windows were lined up. Frank looked over. Two cops sat inside the cruiser. The window was open, and the passenger side cop was leaning on his arm, out the window. Frank's window was down, and he hesitated, his foot hovering over the gas.

The cop opened his mouth and shouted over the wind and sirens. "Get outta the fuckin' way when you see the police, you idiot!" yelled the cop. Confusion washed over Frank's face. The cruiser pulled away and sped off ahead. Frank lifted off the gas and the van slowed down. The cruiser disappeared two intersections ahead, making a left through the red light.

"Holy fuck," Steve muttered.

"What the fuck! What a dick! I was in the right lane! Fuckin' asshole cop!" Frank yelled out. He stretched his hand forward and gave the cop car the finger, but it was well out of sight by the time he did.

"So, we freaked for nothing," Steve said.

"No," said Jack, "you freaked for nothing."

"*Me*? You wanted to run!" Steve yelled back.

"Bro, I was calm. You were all 'let's pull over,'" said Jack calmly.

"Oh, fuck off," said Steve leaning back. "Frank, get us to the lot, and stay outta the way from cops, yeah?"

Frank brushed the beads of sweat off his forehead. He wasn't sure if they were from stress or the heat. He sighed, pressed his foot back down on the gas, and exhaled a deep breath.

Thirteen

Frank pulled into the six-storey parking garage on Lake Shore just east of Spadina. He slowed the van down and took the turns carefully as he drove the trio up to the fifth level. Cars were scattered around the lot, like a giant had just thrown a handful of them around and wherever they landed, they stayed. Each level was populated by roughly the same number of cars, but the place looked empty.

Frank pulled up to the orange pillar marked 5A and parked. "Any word from Kev?" he asked Jack, who was opening his door.

"Nope," Jack said as he pushed the door open and swung his legs out of the van, landing with a thud on the paved asphalt of the lot. He arched his back and flexed every muscle in his body. "Couldn't you get more comfortable seats, Frank? I'm all stiff."

Steve opened the side door and climbed out, "Aren't you always stiff?" he said with a smirk.

"Yeah, but it's only a problem when there aren't any girls around," Jack said, giving Steve a shot in the arm. They both chuckled as they walked around to the front of the van.

The smell of the lake wafted through the night air and mixed with the smell of the exhaust and asphalt of the parking structure. It was a distinct smell but they were used to it, living in Toronto. Just like the smell of rotten eggs that occasionally wafted up from the subway grates in the streets, it caught you off-guard for a second and then you were used to it. Frank looked at his phone. 11:13 pm. They had arranged to meet at this spot at eleven, but the unexpected janitor at the library delayed them. Frank knew why they were late, but neither he, nor Jack nor Steve, knew why Kev wasn't there waiting for them. "Where is he?" Frank said aloud to no one in particular. He reached into his pocket and pulled out his pack of smokes. He shook one out, lit it, and drew a long breath from it. The smoke hit his lungs, swirled and left as he exhaled. A calmness swept over his body and mind. Frank took another drag from the cigarette, exhaled, and leaned back against the front of the van.

"I dunno, man," said Steve. He paced back and forth across the parking spots in front of them, his arms crossed and head down. "Maybe he had problems with the woman? Maybe someone spotted him?"

"No way," said Jack, "he's way too careful for that. He doesn't slip up. He plans out his video game movements. Who does that?" Jack said with a laugh. "No, don't worry, he'll be here. Maybe he just needed gas, or was hungry."

"Hungry?!" said Steve. "He was hungry? On a night like this, he just pulled over for a burger?!" Steve said impatiently.

"Or pizza," Jack said with a smile.

Steve glared back. "It's been like twenty minutes. He should be here. Call him," he said.

Jack scratched the back of his neck and pulled out his phone. Just as he was entering Kev's number, an engine rev echoed through the parking structure. All three men turned their heads towards the ramp leading down to the next level. Headlights lit up the walls and ground, and a VW Golf turned up the ramp. It drove towards them and parked in the space next to them. Kev got out.

"Howdy boys. Sorry to keep you waiting. Got a little hungry on the way," Kev said with a smile. Steve frowned at Kev and then looked over at Jack who grinned and flicked up his eyebrows in an 'I told you so' manner. Steve just shook his head.

"All right, fine. Well, you're here now," said Steve.

"So, I guess since you guys are here, it all went well?"

Jack walked over to Kev and slapped him on the back. "No problem, bro! Off without a hitch!" Steve looked at Jack and cocked an eyebrow. "Okay," said Jack, "not exactly without a hitch, but the bumps we made were smoothed over with bullets and fire."

"What?" Kev asked.

Frank tossed the butt of his cigarette on the floor and ground it into the asphalt with the toe of his boot. "There was a janitor who scared Jack," said Frank.

"He didn't scare me. Just, startled me. So, he kinda got shot," Jack said.

"Okay," Kev said slowly, trying to picture in his head how everything had gone down.

"So Jackie-boy got scared and shot him," Frank said smiling as he teased Jack with the nickname, "and then we couldn't exactly let the librarian live since he saw Jack shoot, so we killed him too. Then set the place alight."

"Yeah," said Jack, "if there was evidence, we killed it with fire."

Kev smiled. "And I assume you got the folio? Where is it?"

Steve went back into the van and pulled out the duffle bag with the folio in it. He unzipped the bag and held it open for Kev to see.

"Hmm. Six million dollars doesn't look like much these days, does it?" Kev said with a laugh.

"As long as it's six million or more, I don't give a shit what it looks like," said Frank.

"Fuckin' A!" chimed in Steve and Jack at the same time.

"So how did it go for you at the wife's house?" Steve said as he zipped up the bag and put it back into the van.

"Uhh, yeah, it went good," said Kev hesitantly. "Did what I needed to do," he said as he shot a quick glance to Frank who met his eyes and gave the slightest of nods.

"Perfect. So, what now?" said Jack.

"Well, we gotta sell this thing," said Steve. "Frank, you talked to Tony? He got a buyer?"

"I saw him the other day, said he was looking into it. Might have a few possible buyers by now. I'll call him tomorrow. Hopefully, we can unload this thing in a day or two," Frank said.

"Sounds good," said Jack. Steve nodded, agreeing with Jack and Frank.

"What if we held on to it for a little while?" Kev asked.

"What do you mean? Why hold on to it? Don't you want money?" Jack asked.

"Well, yeah I do, but what if we hold on to it so that we get more?" Kev said.

"How do we do that?" Jack asked. "How does that work?"

"Well," Kev explained, "we just wait until the value of the folio grows. Like, you know in World War Two when there were all kinds of paintings and sculptures that went missing? The Nazis took them when they invaded towns and cities. They kept it all in vaults and shit like that. Personal Nazi treasure, right? And what happened to those pieces? They were eventually found years and years later, and the pieces that were once thought lost forever, existed again, and their value shot through the roof because they were one of a kind items."

"Okay, I'm not sure if you are making sense or are a complete idiot," Steve said. "You want to hold onto this thing for what, like thirty years? I think we need money now."

"I'm not saying thirty years. I'm saying like a week or two. You said you burned the place, right? It all went up in flames?" Kev asked. The three partners in front of him nodded.

"Okay, so when they go through the ashes and rubble, what will they find? Or rather, what will they not find? The folio. It will be thought to be lost to the fire. Engulfed in the flames. And the buyers that Tony has lined up will be distraught. They thought they had a genuine historical antique, but now they have nothing. Until, a few days after, Tony gives them info that the folio has survived. Now it is in higher demand. The buyers know that the rest of the world thinks it was lost, so the value skyrockets. We could double our earnings here!"

"I still don't know," said Steve. "It's a bit risky holding on to this thing."

"Yeah, but what if he's right?" said Jack.

Frank was halfway through his second cigarette when he finally added to the conversation. "Yeah, what if he's right? I could use a few extra million. Maybe we don't wait too long, but we can have Tony talk to the buyers and tell them that there was this item he almost had, but it was lost in the fire, right? They get all interested and shit and then when they are drooling over the thought of 'oh man, what if I had that thing,' we offer it up at twice the value."

"Exactly, Frank! Exactly!" said an excited Kev.

"That sounds worth trying to me," said Jack. He, Kev, and Frank turned to look at Steve, who stood in front of them, arms crossed and head down, thinking about the whole situation.

"All right," Steve agreed. "Let's do it. Frank, make the call to Tony. Just tell him he can get a bit of a bigger cut if he plays along with it all. Otherwise, why would he do it?"

"Done. I'll call him now," Frank said. He tossed his burnt out cigarette to the ground, pulled out his phone, and walked away from the group to make the call.

"This is it, boys!" Kev exclaimed, clapping his hands. "This is the big break we all need. Oh man, when I get that money, am I going to have fun!"

"Hookers to play video games with?" Jack said laughing. Kev punched him in the chest, and Jack staggered back.

"It better work, man," Steve said. "If we lost the buyers' interest and are stuck with this thing, I'm going to kick your ass," said Steve.

"Don't worry, man! Just like tonight, it'll all go smooth!" Kev could hardly contain his excitement. "I'm just going to bum a smoke off Frank." He walked over to Frank as Jack and Steve began to discuss what they would do with their millions. Kev walked in front of Frank and motioned for a cigarette. Frank handed Kev his pack of smokes with his free hand just as he was ending the call.

"Okay, so Tony wi—" Frank started, but Kev cut him off.

"Fuck that right now," he said to a confused Frank. "Look, I shot the wife."

"We had discussed that. You were okay doing that if we needed to."

"Yeah, I know, but I didn't need to."

"Yes, you did. You had to. No way we could let her live. We killed the librarian and no way she could live after she was part of the whole thing as a hostage."

"Yeah, yeah, you're right."

"It played out well though. It all looked like an accident. How'd you make her death look?"

"Like someone shot her. Police can figure domestic disturbance, and then hubby flew off into the night. They won't find his body or at least identify it right?"

"Yeah, he's ashes by now. You got rid of her body?"

"Yeah. She's just like her husband."

"Good. See, nothing to worry about. Just don't mention it to the other two."

"What do you mean? Why not? Shouldn't they know?"

"Well, Steve took exception to killing the librarian. He was all pissed and didn't want to do it."

"But it had to be done. He knows that, doesn't he? Same with the wife. They both had to go."

"Well, yeah, he gets it, but he doesn't like it. Besides, what he doesn't know can't hurt him. It's all taken care of, so it'll be fine."

"Okay. So, it's all good?"

"It's all good," Frank said with a smile. Kev smiled

back as the two returned to the van.

"What're you two smiling about?" Jack asked.

"Tony's going to do it, right Frank?" Kev said.

"Yeah. He's in for some more money too. Hardly took convincing, unlike you, Steve," Frank said smiling.

"Well, you can all smack me with your stacks of cash if this works out," said Steve.

"All right, I'm going to hold on to the folio for now," said Frank. "I got the family, and I'll just hide it in one of the kids' rooms.

The other three agreed. No point in making a stupid argument about who should hold onto it or anything like that. Waste of time and energy. They all trusted each other anyway. It wasn't like those heist movies where there was a new guy added to the team at the last minute, and the whole heist was full of tricks and betrayals. They had each other's backs.

"Well boys," said Kev, "looks like another one for the books. I'm getting outta here."

"We'll meet up in a couple of days, discuss where we are with the buyers," said Frank.

"Cool," said Kev. He shook everyone's hand. "Well done, boys. We did it." Kev got into his car, and it roared to life as he turned it on. He pulled forward through the empty spaces and drove off down the ramp, the sound of his engine trailing off into the night. Frank, Jack, and Steve got back into the van.

"Oh man, I'm excited about waiting for money," said Jack. "Does that even make sense?"

"No idea, but I know exactly what you mean," Steve said. "All thanks to this," he said patting the duffle bag with the folio in it.

"All right boys, time to take you home," Frank said as he drove out of parking garage into the night.

Fourteen

Two days had passed since the foursome left the parking garage on Lake Shore. Each kept to himself, lying low. They stayed at home and kept their eyes and ears on the news. The fire at the library was big news, covered by all of the local stations. The reports showed the building burning and said more than eighty percent of the books inside were lost in the fire. There was no mention of any bodies found in the remains of the fire. The fire department had yet to find the cause but believed it to be arson. There was no evidence, no leads pointing to any perpetrator. As far as the officials knew, the foursome who did it didn't exist, and the men were pleased with that. They knew they were almost in the clear. They just had to sell the folio.

Their plan was to wait two days and then meet up. Frank had set the sale process in motion the night of the heist with the call he placed to Tony, and he was to call him back this morning to hear if there was any progress. Depending on what was happening with buyers, they would meet up and discuss whether to make a sale or hold out longer.

Steve sat on his bed in his apartment. It was almost noon, and he had been awake since ten, but he lacked the motivation to get out of bed. Instead, he sat up, propped against his pillow with his laptop, watching episodes of *Top*

Gear. Steve wasn't a "true petrol head" as the hosts of the show would say, but he liked the show and could appreciate cars from Ferraris to Lamborghinis to Astons. Since the heist, he had gone back and watched a handful of episodes featuring some of the cars he thought he would be able to afford with his cut of the money, but he was careful. Steve wasn't sure if he should spend huge amounts right away. *Wouldn't that be suspicious?* he had thought to himself

He was just finishing up an episode when his phone rang. The caller ID displayed Frank's name. "Yeah?" Steve answered.

"Meet tonight, at the pub, seven," said Frank.

"Okay," said Steve and hung up. He tossed his phone to his side and rested his head back on his pillow. The next stage would be back at the beginning point of this plan. Back to the pub where they originally planned the heist. "Gotta keep up appearances, I guess," said Steve to himself out loud. Then he settled back into bed to watch another episode on his laptop.

❖

Frank made calls to Kev and Jack after he hung up with Steve. Both said they would be there. Frank wandered in his house from room to room. He was antsy, nervous. They had never done something this big before. They had dealt with Tony Jones on previous occasions. He was a solid guy, a bit shady, but you came to expect that when working with someone who dealt under the table in the black market. There was some history between Tony and Frank. All good as the two had dealt with each other many times, and Frank had even gotten his wife's engagement ring through Tony, but there was some bad blood through the group. Tony didn't like Jack and had almost killed him. All a misunderstanding according to Jack, but Frank knew better, and so did Tony. If the two were ever left in a room together, neither would make it out alive.

After a robbery, Jack and Frank had gone to see Tony, Jack for the first time, at Tony's pawn shop. When they walked in the door, Tony pulled his shotgun from below the counter screaming at Jack to "Get the fuck out," or he would "shoot his fucking head off!" Jack backed up out of the store saying he'd wait outside and Frank stayed behind.

"What the hell was that about?" Frank asked Tony.

"That little bitch. Fuck him. You deal with him? I ain't dealin' with him, Frank. We go back a ways but I ain't dealin' with that ma'fucka," Tony said pointing towards the door.

"What the hell happened, man? He cheat you or something?"

"Yeah, fuck that bitch cheated me! Cheated my girl on me!" Tony said with rage in his eyes.

Frank looked confused. "I'm not even sure what that means."

"It means that little punk fucked my girl! I came home one night, after a long day, y'know. Lookin' forward to seein' mah girl. So I walk in the place, and I hear her moanin' and the bed movin', and I rush into the bedroom to see what's up and there is that fucker bangin' mah girl! I tell ya, I startled the hell outta both of 'em! And he ran like hell when I went for the bat I have in the closet. I think he barely grabbed his clothes and got out, but I took some swings.

Broke a damn lamp. I'll kill him, man, swore I would if I ever saw him again!" Tony explained in a yell.

"Well, fuck sakes, Tony. You gotta let that go. I work with him. He's a good kid. Bit dumb at times, but he does what he needs to get a job done. And isn't it the fault of your girl? How could he know, maybe she didn't tell him about you," Frank replied.

"Hell no, Frank. You do not blame mah girl! Do not bring her into this. It is all that punk bitch's fault!" Tony yelled.

"Okay, okay. You still goin' to deal with me?" Frank asked.

"Yeah. Just don't bring that asshole here no more. Got that?"

Frank never took Jack there again, and from then on, Jack stayed away from the business of fencing. He just waited until Frank brought them their money. Frank asked Jack about it once after that day and Jack gave him the same story, but added that the girl said she was single and lived with her brother, so any guy things around the house were his. "I figured, why would she lie about that?" Jack had said innocently.

Frank chuckled to himself, thinking back about it as he pulled into a parking spot outside the Foxhound. He was, once again, the first one to arrive. He got out of his van, and as he sauntered over to the front door of the pub, he pulled out his smokes and lit one up. He leaned against the wall to the left of the entrance and puffed away.

The night was cooling down after another hot day, but Frank was still sweating through his clothes. The air was thick and humid. His shirt was damp under the arms and in the middle of his chest and back. He pulled at the neckline and fluttered the shirt to get some cool air circulating. He wiped his forehead with the back of his hand, pushing the sweat to one side where it beaded and dripped down his eyebrow into his eye. The sweat stung, and he wiped his eyes with his fingers. He cursed at the heat as he took another drag from his cigarette. He tossed the butt to the sidewalk and ground it with the toe of his boot. Lit up a second smoke. As he tilted his head back up after lighting the tip, he saw Steve pulling into the parking lot in his pickup truck. Frank waited by the door and finished his cigarette in three quick drags as Steve approached him.

"Hey man," said Steve. Frank nodded back. "We the only ones here?" Frank nodded again. "Well, if you're done getting cancer," Steve said, gesturing towards the door. Frank smirked and walked through the door.

They walked into the bar, the floor creaking under their feet. It was pretty empty, and the two walked to their usual booth. They sat down opposite each other, each placing his wallet, keys, and phone on the table. "Too damn uncomfortable in the pockets," Frank said. Steve leaned back against the wall of the booth and surveyed the bar. There was a couple at a table sharing drinks and talking, sitting close to each other, probably on a date. There was a small group at another table in a corner, five people, two girls, and three guys, having a laugh, telling stories, and drinking away. Several people sat at the bar, pints in their hands and heads tilted up at the TVs on the wall behind the bar, above the shelves of liquor. Steve's eyes made their way back to the front door where he saw Kev walk in. Steve waved at him, and Kev walked over to their table. Steve shuffled over, and Kev slid into the booth.

"Still waiting on Jack, I assume," Kev said while cracking his knuckles.

"Yeah. Guess he's a bit late, but I'm not waiting to order. I'm thirsty! This heat is brutal," Steve said.

"Yeah, eh?" said Kev. "My place has no air conditioning and I'm dying. I have, like, four fans on but it's still hot as hell in there."

"Nothing a cold beer can't fix," Frank said with a chuckle.

Becky walked over to them from behind the bar. She looked good as usual in her miniskirt, tight, low-cut top and high leather boots that showed off her long slender legs. The three guys could hardly keep from staring at her.

"Hey, boys," she said in a sultry voice, "where's Jack? You guys finally ditch him?" she added with a laugh.

"Nah, he's just running late," said Steve.

"Oh, that's weird. He usually comes early," Becky said, chuckling to herself at the double entendre that only she caught. "Well, while you wait, what can I get for you?"

Frank, Kev, and Steve exchanged looks before Frank said, "Ummm, a pitcher of Coors and a plate of nachos." Kev and Steve nodded.

"Okey-dokey," Becky said. "Back in a bit." She turned away with a smile and all three men sitting in the booth watched her walk away.

"Damn," said Steve. Kev just nodded, and Frank shook himself back to reality. Frank checked his phone. "Okay, where is Jack?" he asked out loud.

"He responded to your message earlier today, right?" asked Kev.

"Yeah. Just said *ok* but that's enough to know that he read it," Frank explained.

"Idiot probably fell asleep," Steve said with a smile. "Try calling him again."

Frank dialled Jack's number and held the phone to his ear. It rang several times and then reached his voicemail. He ended the call and dialled again. Same result. "Well, now he's just not answering. It's ringing, but he ain't pickin' up."

"Whatever, maybe he left his phone somewhere," Kev suggested. At that moment Becky arrived with their beer and three glasses. She put the four items on the table and left.

"Okay, well forget Jack for now," Steve said as he poured the golden liquid into the three glasses, handing the first to Frank, the second to Kev, and keeping the third for himself. The pitcher was wet with condensation and left a wet ring on the table underneath it. Steve licked his lips, anticipating the taste of the cold beer and took a satisfying sip. "Oh, that's fresh," he said, wiping his lips. He felt the cold liquid run through his body, cooling him down from the heat of the air. "Okay, Frank, so what word is there from Tony?"

"He called, and he has a couple 'interested parties' as he said. So it looks like the plan sorta worked," Frank said.

"I knew it, man! Didn't I tell you it would?" Kev said, grinning ear to ear.

"Okay, okay. For now, yeah, you were right," said Steve, "but what are they offering? Did you get a number?"

"No. He didn't have anything like that. Just said that there's a couple of guys that would be interested in the item.

Well, would be if it survived the fire," Frank said with a wink.

"Well, there's always a chance," said Kev, returning the wink.

"Okay, stop winking. It's freakin' me out," said Steve with a laugh.

Frank took a big gulp of his drink and said, "Even if there is no number, we know that it will be at least the six million. I know that Tony said that much to them as the original starting point, and knowing him, he probably started doin' what he does and planting ideas that it's more valuable and all that shit so that he gets the price up. He knows, the higher the price it goes for, the more we can give him."

"Yeah man, sounds good. Sounds like classic Tony. Just wants his cut and wants it as big as possible," Steve said.

"Okay, so what do we want to do now?" Kev asked.

"It seems to me that Tony might have two buyers, right?" Steve asked

"Yeah," agreed Kev and Frank.

"We could have a bit of a bidding war. Run the price up really high. Get Tony to say that there is another person interested and offering more. You know, standard sales tactics," Steve said smiling.

"Makes sense to me," said Kev.

"All right. I'll tell Tony to do that," Frank said. He stepped out of the booth and walked to an empty corner of the pub to make the call.

"This is going to work out amazingly," Kev said. "You know, I was a little worried, but this is working out better than I thought."

"Yeah, I know! So smooth! Of course, we are professionals," Steve said slyly, smirking out of the side of his mouth.

"But where is Jack?" Kev asked, checking his phone to see the time. "It's weird that he's this late. It's almost eight now. Where is he? I'll try calling him."

"Yeah. Maybe he forgot?"

"How can he forget something like this?" Kev said pressing the call button and pressing the phone to his ear. A minute passed and Kev ended the call saying, "Still not picking up. Maybe he's asleep or something. Well, whatever, just try to call him tomorrow and fill him in I guess."

"Yeah. No point in worrying too much now. Probably nothing anyway," Steve said. Frank returned to the table and eased himself slowly into the bench seat, the cushion exhaling with a wheeze as he plopped his large mass down.

"What'd Tony have to say?" Steve asked.

"He's good for the plan," said Frank, taking a swig from his glass, finishing the remaining beer.

Becky arrived and slid the plate of nachos onto the table between the trio. "Still no Jack?" she asked.

"Nope," replied Steve.

"Oh well," she said with a slight sigh. She hadn't seen him since the day after the burning incident, and he had barely responded to her texts. She hoped he was okay, or at least healed enough that they could get together again. She pictured him in her head and smiled. She caught herself picturing them having sex and snapped back to reality. "So," she said grabbing the empty pitcher, "ready for another one?"

Frank nodded along with the other two. Becky smiled and walked away.

"Any word from Jack?" Frank asked.

"Nah," Kev said, "I just tried calling but no response. I'll try him again tomorrow."

"Yeah, all right," agreed Frank.

They settled in for the night, drinking their beers and eating nachos. They ordered more food as the night went on. The bar never got busy and by eleven-thirty, the place was nearly empty. They were ready to leave, so they called over Becky to settle up. She brought their bill, and each of them threw down some cash. They got up to leave when Frank's phone went off. He answered it.

"Hello? Yeah, Tony," Frank said walking back to the same corner he had used for his call earlier that night. Kev and Steve exchanged glances of confusion and eagerness. Maybe Tony was calling because one of the buyers had an offer. At least, they hoped it was that sort of conversation and not the kind where Tony tells them that they now have no buyers. Kev and Steve walked towards the front door signalling to Frank that they would wait outside. Frank nodded as he made eye contact with them and turned back to focus on his call.

A few minutes later, Frank joined them. The night had cooled down considerably and the air was now crisp, all humidity had vanished. The sky was clear save for a few wispy clouds strafing the starry sky. The moon lit up the treetops and buildings. Frank stepped through the door out into the air and immediately pulled out a cigarette.

"Good news, boys," Frank said as he lit one up, "looks like we have a solid buyer who wants the folio and is willing to offer around ten mil." Frank spoke nonchalantly, as though the amount was nothing to him.

"Are you fucking kidding?!" yelled Kev. He fist pumped the air. "Haha! I knew it!"

"Yeah, yeah, good for you, Kev," Steve said. He looked back at Frank. "Okay, so what do we need to do?"

"We need to meet up tomorrow. Four of us. Tony is going to talk to the other buyer either later tonight or tomorrow. Then he'll call me, let me know what's up, and we can go see him."

"Sounds fucking good to me!" said Kev. "Holy shit, ten million! Can you believe that?!"

"That is just fucking awesome," exclaimed Steve.

Frank finished up his cigarette. "Well, I'm fuckin' tired, so I'm goin' home to dream of a few million dollars," he said chuckling. "I'll call you guys tomorrow." Frank walked to his van giving a short, quick wave.

"Yeah, I'm doing the same. Night, man," said Kev.

"Later," said Steve. They walked to their cars, got in, and drove home. Each was grinning the biggest grin he had ever had, thinking about how perfectly the plan had worked out. They just had to share the news with Jack.

Fifteen

Steve had been sitting in his apartment all afternoon wearing nothing but boxers, and watching movies when his phone rang. Frank had called to tell him to meet up at Tony's pawn shop. Frank said he had news that the buyer was interested, so they were going to meet with Tony in person to discuss it. The other guys would meet them there too.

"Even Jack?" Steve asked with a chuckle, knowing the history between Jack and Tony.

"If he shows, but he'll just stay outside. He's scared shitless of Tony," Frank said laughing on the other end, "but that's if he shows. I still can't get a hold of him, and today, before I called you, I couldn't get through to Kev either. His phone didn't even ring."

"Really? Maybe the battery died. Not sure why Jack would still not be picking up."

"I dunno what's wrong with these guys sometimes."

"It's not like they've done this before. It's not in their character. I'm pretty sure they want this as much as we do. Wait," Steve said thinking, a look of shock washing over his face, "you don't think. . .Police?"

"No way," Frank replied. "We were clean in and out. Same with Kev. Besides, haven't you kept your eyes on the news? They said arson but no actual leads. They're thinking it was, like, pissed-off students or some shit like that. We are in the clear, man."

"Yeah. Right. Okay. But still, it doesn't sit right that they aren't answering their phones. Maybe we should check in on them?"

"Yeah. Okay, if you want to. We can go after we meet with Tony. But I'm not blowing him off for nothing."

"It's not nothing when half the team is missing!" Steve cried back. He was pacing his room, kicking the shirts and pants lying on the floor. His heart was beating a little faster now as his mind raced through the possibilities of what could have happened to Kev and Jack.

Maybe the police did find something. Maybe something had been traced back to one of them. Maybe they picked up Jack and he gave up Kev, or just found each of them individually. Steve's breathing got heavier with each thought. What if the police were on the way to get him too?!

Frank heard Steve's breathing get heavier and tried to calm him down. "Look, relax man. It's all okay. Nothing on the news."

"They don't always report everything on the news!" Steve interrupted, "Like, if they know it was a team, and they don't want the other members to get spooked and run for it, they won't release anything to the press! That's how they do things, man! That's how they catch people! Don't you watch TV or movies? Fuck!"

"Fuckin' calm down! It's nothing! Look we'll go to their places after we meet with Tony, okay? We'll check things out, and it will be fine. Jack's probably just holed up with a girl, and Kev's in some Nintendo tournament or some shit. Fuckin' relax."

Steve took a couple of deep breaths, exhaling long and

slow. "Okay," he whispered.

"Okay." He began to feel calmer. "I'll see you at Tony's."

"Good. In an hour. See you then." Frank hung up.

Steve tossed his phone on the bed. He walked to his bathroom. He was sweating, but not just because his room was hot. He was feeling the heat of their position. They had to move the folio. They couldn't hold onto it much longer. If the cops were getting close somehow, they needed to get rid of the evidence. They didn't have anything left from that night other than the folio itself. Once it was gone, they would have money instead.

Steve leaned over the bathroom sink, turned on the cold water, and let it run for a few seconds. He cupped his hands under the tap, collected the cold water, and splashed it over his face several times. He ran his fingers through his hair, pushing it off his forehead, now damp with the cool water. He felt refreshed. He looked at himself in the mirror. "Okay, buddy," he said to himself, "just calm the fuck down. It's okay. It's all good. Keep it together." He dried his face with a towel and went to his bedroom to get dressed.

❖

An hour later Steve pulled into the little plaza near Dufferin and Lawrence. It was a small strip mall that consisted of a convenience store, a Chinese take-out, laundromat, and Tony's pawnshop.

Steve pulled into a spot next to Frank's van. How was he always first to arrive, Steve wondered. He got out and walked around to the driver side of Frank's van. Frank was leaning out the window, puffing on a cigarette.

"Those things are going to kill you, man," Steve said.

"Yeah, I know, but it's slow. I'll have time to spend my money, don't you worry." Frank flicked the butt to the ground and Steve backed up as Frank opened his door.

"Still no word from Jack or Kev?" Steve asked. "I tried calling a couple of times, but nothing."

"Yeah, same," Frank said. They walked to the pawn-shop.

The coolness from the night was gone. The sky was covered with a thick blanket of dark grey clouds. Steve looked up at them as they walked across the lot and felt a drop of rain hit his cheek. He wiped it away as they stepped onto the curb and opened the door to Tony's shop.

The store wasn't very big and it was crammed with product. The wall to their right as they walked in had the counter and jewellery cases along the length. Behind it were paintings and other wall decorations, all with price tags in the corners. The wall to their left featured the electronics: televisions, radios, sound systems, speakers, computers, video games, and a few guitars. The front window was barred with iron. Displayed in the windows were neon signs and card signs that offered deals and lists of items sold in the store. Tony was smart enough not to put anything in the actual windows so that there was nothing obvious to steal. There were a couple of bicycles, two lounge chairs, and some old, worn desks stuffed beside the cases. In between all these items were bins and boxes of smaller items that people had brought in. Steve looked at it all and couldn't figure out who the hell would buy any of it.

They walked up to the counter and just as they got there, Tony rose up as if from nowhere. He had been crouched on the floor sorting through another box of junk.

"Hey Tony," Frank said.

"Frank!" Tony exclaimed, reaching out a hand, "was wonderin' if you was even gonna show up!"

"I'm on time," said Frank coolly.

"Hey, man," Steve said, "good to see you again."

"Yeah man, f'show. Steve, right? Aha, I knew it. I only seen ya a couple of times but, yeah, I recognize," Tony said, offering his hand to Steve who shook it. "Just the two of you? You got that fucker Jack waiting outside?" Tony said with a mean look in his eye.

"Still can't let it go, eh?" Frank chuckled. "Don't worry, he ain't here."

"Good. I don't wanna have to waste no bullets on his ass," said Tony with a smile. He walked to the front of the store and flipped the latch to lock the door.

"Why does he talk that way?" Steve whispered to Frank.

"I dunno, I think he does it on purpose. Thinks it makes him tougher or some shit. He never used to be all 'gangsta,'" said Frank, making good use of air quotes, "but he started, and I didn't call him on it because I thought it was hilarious. Now it's annoying," Frank whispered, cutting himself off as Tony came back to them. Steve stifled a laugh and tried to hide his smile.

"Okay, follow me, boys," said Tony. Steve and Frank followed him through the door into the quiet, tiny, back room. It had a desk and a chair. On the desk was a laptop and a phone and some papers strewn about. Tony sat down in the chair and swivelled to face Steve and Frank.

"All right. So, here's what's up. I got this buyer who's interested in this book of yours. I got him interested and upped the price, but before I could even suggest that it would be more valuable, he offered up the ten mil."

"Cash?" Frank asked.

"Nah, man, this guy does wire transfers. Keeps all that shit clean and hidden, y'know? Going through accounts in the Caymans and shit like that. Dude is legit, sneak." Steve raised his eyebrows and scratched his face to hide his smile at Tony's lingo. "So, whatchu guys think?"

"Well, what's the word on that second buyer?" Steve asked, crossing his arms. "He make the same kind of offer?"

"Nah, hadn't heard from him in a while. This first guy was most interested, though. The other guy saw it as, like, an investment or somethin' but this first guy, he is down. He wants it."

"Okay, so how about we counter offer him, raise the price?" Steve suggested.

"Yeah, I could do that. Whatchu thinkin'?" Steve looked over at Frank who met his eyes. Both stood with their arms crossed over their chests.

"Twelve million?" they both said at the same time.

"Damn, you guys think alike!" Tony said with a laugh. "All right, I'll call him now. Not sure he'll answer, though. Usually, goes through a couple people or machines to get to him, but let's see." Tony turned back to the desk and reached for the phone, leaned back, and pulled out a little book from of his pocket. He leafed through several pages until he found the right one about halfway through. He dialled the number and waved at Steve and Frank to leave the room. They opened the door and stepped back out into the store.

A couple of minutes later Tony's arm waved them back inside.

"Okay, so he said yes," Tony said.

"Wow really? That was fucking easy," said Steve with disbelief.

"Should've aimed higher, dammit," said Frank. "Think we can try again?"

"I wouldn't," said Tony, "as much as I want you to make more money, so that I get more money, this guy agreed to your deal, so you gotta accept that. Otherwise, it's bad man, like, ill faith and that shit. The guy could get pissed and just peace out, no deal."

"Yeah, Frank. More is always nicer, but that's a fucking deal we got there. Twelve million. Fuck sakes, that's a lot."

"So, we gots a deal then?" Tony asked, leaning back in his chair stretching out his arms. Frank looked at Steve, and they both nodded. "Saahweeet!" Tony yelled as he jumped forward in the chair and clapped his hands together loudly.

"So what now? How do we go about doing this, making the transfer?" Frank asked.

"He gave me this email, and once I email him stating that we gots a deal, he's gonna make an account and give us the info but not the password. He'll transfer the money, email me a screenshot of the account with the balance of the twelve million, and then send a guy to pick up the folio in the next day or two. The guy he sends will have the password for the bank account, so we can take the money."

"Wow, that's a pretty good plan. Thorough. Safe. Sounds good," said Steve. Frank nodded in agreement.

"Okay, boys, then I'll get this shit started! I'll call Frank when I get word that the pickup man is here, and then you boys can come and get your money. Bring that book of yours too, hah! Don't be forgettin' that now!"

"Great stuff, man," said Frank. "Thanks," he said, reaching out his hand to shake Tony's.

"Yeah, Tony, thanks a lot," said Steve, shaking Tony's hand too.

"No problemo boys. Just don't thank me with words and hands. Thank me by handing me my cut of the cash," Tony said, a white-toothed grin spreading across his face. He got up out of the chair and walked to the entrance of the store. He unlocked and held open the door. Steve and Frank passed through. "Be in touch," he said, closing the door behind them.

"Fuckin' sick!" Steve yelled pumping his fist into the air.

"Twelve million, damn," said Frank.

They walked over to their cars and Frank lit up a cigarette on the way. He took a long drag and puffed the smoke out in front of him. It wafted over in front of Steve who coughed and fanned away the smoke.

Steve pulled out his phone. Still no new messages or calls. Frank did the same with the same result. No word from Kev or Jack. Neither had shown up to the store, and neither had made any communication.

"Okay, we're done here. Now we go check on these two, yeah?" Steve asked.

"Yeah. Jack first. See you there," said Frank as he slammed his driver door shut.

Sixteen

Steve pulled up to the back parking lot of Jack's apartment building. For once, Frank was not the first to arrive. Steve pulled into a spot and turned off his truck. He got out and sat on the hood. A couple of minutes later Frank pulled in and parked next to him.

"Still no answer," Steve said as Frank got out of his van.

"Well, let's see what the hell is going on," said Frank, slamming his door shut.

Jack's building rose up in front of them, thirty storeys high. It was charcoal grey and white brick, with black half-walls bordering each balcony. Some balconies had barbeques, chairs or plants, while others were bare.

"Wait!" exclaimed Steve. "How the hell are we supposed to get in. It's all locked, and he has to buzz us in."

"Easy," said Frank. He walked up to the entrance and hit the buzzers for almost every apartment. Voices came through the intercom and in between the voices they heard the buzz and click of the front door lock. "Someone is always waiting for someone," Frank said, smiling and pulling open the door.

They walked in and down the first few steps into the lobby. It was empty. The floor was carpeted, and there was a small grouping of chairs with a coffee table on the left.

On the right was a door to the stairs and the mailboxes for the tenants, and ahead was the hallway leading to the elevators, one set of doors on each side. They walked towards the elevators and pressed for one to come. The button glowed orange, and they watched the digital display above the door count down from fifteen to the ground. The doors opened, and they stepped inside. Steve pressed twenty-two and the doors slid closed.

They rode the slow elevator to the twenty-second floor and stepped out into the grey hallway. It was carpeted just as the lobby was, and fixtures overhead lit up the hallway every ten feet.

They walked down the hallway to Jack's apartment; it was quiet except for their muffled footsteps and Steve's heavy breathing.

"What're you, out of breath?" Frank muttered. Steve ignored him and carried on. He was trying to think of what waited for them inside Jack's apartment. What if he wasn't there?

Then what did they do?

They reached his apartment door, and knocked. No answer. Steve rapped his knuckles again on the solid wooden door, but still, there was no response. He looked at Frank who shrugged. Steve tried the knob. It twisted, and the door swung open.

A foul smell hit their nostrils and turned Steve's stomach into knots. Frank coughed and turned away from the door.

"What the fuck!" Steve said as he coughed into his hand. He pulled his shirt up over his nose and mouth to try to block the smell from invading his nose any further.

"Idiot leave the fridge open or somethin'? Fuck!" Frank

said. "It smells like old steaks that went bad."

"Eh! Jack! You in here?" Steve said walking into the apartment. Frank entered behind him and closed the door.

The apartment was a good size. A small hallway ran down the middle of the apartment opening into a living room. On the right were doors to the bathroom and bedroom, and to the left was the kitchen. Small, but comfortable for a bachelor.

Frank walked into the kitchen and Steve went straight into the living room. Both rooms were empty.

"Well, the fridge is closed and there ain't any food out, so that's not food we're smelling. The fuck is that, though?" Frank said, as he too now had his shirt over his mouth and nose.

Steve walked to the bedroom and opened the door. Clothes were strewn all over the floor and bed, and the sheets were a mess. DVD cases lay on the floor in front of the TV that sat at the foot of the bed on a dresser against the wall. But still, no Jack.

They walked to the bathroom, and Steve kicked open the door. He nearly vomited when he saw the scene. He felt his lunch rise into his throat, but he forced it back down. The smell didn't help. It slapped them in the face when they opened the door, like the first scent they got entering the apartment was just a teaser, and now the full aroma exploded.

Bent over the bathtub was Jack. He was half on the floor, half in the tub, his hips resting on the porcelain frame. Blood was spattered all over the wall, and the tub had a pool of red in the bottom. His skin was pale and dry, wrinkled and waxy. His hair was scraggly and messy, falling forward to cover his face. In the back of his head, just above the neck was a hole. A bloody hole left by a bullet. He had been dead for a couple of days, and he was decomposing.

"What. The. Fuck," Frank whispered, his mouth dropping open.

Steve turned back into the room. He began to walk over to the body. "Fuck! FUCK FUCK FUCK! MAN! WHAT THE FUCK!" Steve yelled.

"Shut up!" Frank said harshly, cupping his hand over Steve's mouth, "someone will hear you. We gotta get the fuck outta here."

"What?! No! He's dead, Frank! Who the fuck did this? Why…why would anyone shoot him? We gotta call the cops," he said reaching into his pocket for his phone.

"Fuck no," said Frank. "No way we're calling the cops."

"Why not? We gotta report this!"

"Oh yeah, and have the fucking police sniffing around while we try to sell the fucking folio! Yeah, that's a great idea. Then they start searching for him, and who knows what they find. What if they find some shit, and put other shit together, and then we all go down? Fuck that! I am not going to jail!"

"We can't just leave him here, fuckin' rotting away. He doesn't deserve that!" Steve said, walking towards the body. Frank grabbed him by the waist and pulled him back, out of the bathroom.

"No, you do not touch him. Did you touch anything here? Wipe anything you did with your shirt. Doors or whatever," said Frank as he began wiping down the light switches and any place he remembered touching. "Look, at some point, someone will find him, but there is nothin' we can do now, got that?"

"Oh fuck," Steve said as dread washed over his face. His skin grew pale, and his breathing got heavier and faster. "Fuck," he said again. His hands felt clammy, and he felt sweat begin to form on his forehead and neck.

"What?" Frank asked impatiently. "Come on. We gotta go!" Frank pushed Steve towards the door. Steve's legs didn't want to move, and he almost face planted into the door before he reached out and caught himself. Frank reached around opened the door and pushed Steve into the hallway. He wiped the door where Steve had touched and then wiped the door knob and closed the door. "Okay, I get why you're freaking out, but what else got you pale in there?"

"What about Kev?" Steve asked, his eyes widening and his voice trailing off, barely able to speak his friend's name.

"Oh shit," Frank said, as the same expression washed over his face. "Fuck. Let's go." They dashed down the hallway and scrambled down the stairs. They ran out of the lobby, got in their cars and drove off.

Seventeen

The rain started coming down heavily as Steve and Frank made their way to Kev's apartment. Pedestrians on the street scrambled for cover in shops and bus shelters. Some had left the house prepared and popped open umbrellas while others were unaffected by the downpour and just carried on their way.

The wipers of Steve's truck were working overtime, but they could not match the pace that his heart was racing at. Ever since discovering Jack in that bathroom, Steve's heart had picked up and hadn't slowed down. His breathing was heavy and quick. He swallowed past the lump that had formed in his throat and gripped the steering wheel with white knuckles.

Frank had been so much calmer. *How had he stayed so calm and collected,* Steve wondered. It was like he had seen it all before. *Maybe he was just that sort of person where death, blood, and gore didn't affect him.* Steve knew he was affected and he felt his stomach heave as he pictured Jack's blown open skull, blood and brain splattered over the tiles and tub.

He put a hand to his mouth to keep from throwing up all over his truck.

He was driving right behind Frank, and they turned onto Oxford Street, off Spadina Avenue. They parked against the curb and got out, and the rain was pouring down, soaking them within seconds. Steve blinked the droplets out of his eyes as he met Frank under the awning that covered the front door to Kev's apartment building.

"Buzzer's different here. The plan from last time won't work," said Frank in a raised voice so he could be heard over the rain pounding down from above.

Steve dug around his front pocket for his keys and fingered through them until he found a square-headed silver key. He held it up for Frank to see. "He gave me a spare for emergencies," Steve explained. "I think this counts as one."

Frank nodded. Steve turned to the front door and unlocked it. They walked in and down the narrow hall to the elevator at the end. They rode it up to the third floor and got out. Frank stood calmly in the elevator, waiting patiently to arrive at Kev's floor but Steve was a nervous mess. He paced back and forth, wringing his hands together and cracking his knuckles. When the doors opened, he dashed down the hallway to apartment five. He didn't even knock but put the key in the lock straight away. He swung the door open and stepped in, Frank following close behind. The door slammed behind them as they entered.

"Remember," Frank whispered, "don't touch shit." Steve nodded.

They walked into the small apartment. The kitchen and living room were empty. Nothing looked out of place. The kitchen was clean, not even a dish lying out. The living room was well kept, the wall of video games was neat and tidy, and even the remotes for all the electronics in the room were arranged neatly on the table beside the chair in the middle of the room.

"Does he even live here? It looks like a museum," Frank said in awe at the tidiness.

There was no sign of life and Steve began to wonder if Kev was even here or had come here at all in the last day. He began to doubt that they would find Kev here and started to wonder where they would look next when he opened the bedroom door and, just like when he opened the door to Jack's apartment, the blood drained from his face.

On the bed was Kev. He lay across the width of the bed, his feet hanging off the edge, hovering inches from the floor. Under his feet, on the hardwood floor was a pool of blood. A stream ran down the side of the bed and along Kev's body which rested in a puddle of crimson.

There was a single bullet hole in the middle of his forehead. It looked the same size as the one in Jack's head. Kev's eyes were wide, and his mouth open in shock.

Steve felt tears build up in his eyes, but he blinked them away. He gritted and ground his teeth, fighting back tears, and swung towards the wall. Frank caught his hand just before he slammed it through the drywall. Steve turned to look at Frank who cocked an eyebrow and shook his head, motioning for them to leave.

"We gotta get outta here. We can mourn later," said Frank.

"How can you be so fucking calm?!" Steve yelled, spit flying from his mouth and spraying Frank. Steve shoved him out of the bedroom into the hall. "What the fuck is wrong with you?!

"You're so fucking calm when two of our friends have been killed!"

Frank frowned. "Don't you think I know that? I know

they're dead. I don't like it. They're my friends too, but we gotta remain calm. We can't freak out because otherwise we could end up dead. We just gotta leave and figure this out somewhere else."

"Fuck," Steve muttered, calming his voice. He knew Frank was right. They couldn't hang out here. They had to leave. They had to regroup and figure out their next move. Steve had an uneasy feeling, and not just from seeing his two friends dead in their apartments. Frank was too calm about this all. Steve shook the thought away. No, that doesn't make sense, he thought to himself, but couldn't help his mind from wandering.

They left Kev's apartment the same way they had entered it. They wiped off anything they touched and went back down to the lobby.

"Look," said Frank. "I know this is fucked, but let's just go home and start fresh tomorrow. We can figure it out, but I think we have to put the sale first."

Steve didn't know what to say. He was in shock from seeing the two dead bodies. Two dead friends. His mind was racing over the scenarios in which each died, who did it, and why. In the back of his mind, he had the idea of betrayal. Frank's betrayal. This latest statement didn't help to muffle that idea. Frank wanted the money first, justice second. Steve didn't want Frank to know what he was thinking, so he nodded yes and left for his car. He needed to go home and think things over. Think about what they knew, what they needed to know, and see if there were any connections, and if anything at all made sense.

"Just go home, stay there. We gotta keep quiet until we meet with Tony's buyer tomorrow or the day after. It'll be fine. After we have the money we can decide what to do," Frank said.

"Yeah, okay," said Steve, his mind still whirling with what just happened in the last two hours. He got into his car and sat there, the rain beating down, soaking the world he thought he knew. A thunderclap sounded, and Steve jumped, startled back to reality. He looked at his phone, still clutched in his hand. He had been sitting there motionless for half an hour. Frank was long gone. Steve found his keys in his pocket and started up the car.

Eighteen

The drive home was slow. The rain was still coming down but had lightened up slightly. The roads were scattered with puddles, waves of water went crashing into the gutters when vehicles plowed through them. Steve wanted to get home, but as usual, when anything came from the sky—rain, snow, hell even mist—everyone forgot how to drive. Steve would have been that frustrated driver, yelling at all those around him and blaring his horn, but he was too preoccupied with the events of the last couple of hours. The emotions that he felt ranged from elation to heartbreak, panic to fear.

Steve was plagued with questions about Jack and Kev. What had they been up to, and what might have happened to them? In the back of his mind, Steve had been wondering if they might be dead, but it had seemed so outlandish. Who would want to kill them? The day had progressed into curiosity of a different kind when they met up with Tony, and that curiosity turned into excitement and happiness when the final plans for the sale were outlined and put into effect. Then it all went downhill from there.

The discovery of Jack's body left Steve confused, disgusted, nauseous, and panicked. The discovery of Kev's soon after heightened those feelings, and now on the drive home in the rain, all alone, paranoia was settling in Steve's mind.

He needed to get home. Crack a beer and sit down. Maybe watch a funny movie to calm his mind and nerves. Or jerk off. That always relaxed him.

He looked in his rear-view mirror and saw a red Dodge. He thought he had seen that same car several kilometres back. He began to feel uneasy. It was probably nothing. How many red Dodges are there in the world? Steve still had a feeling that he was being followed. He made a quick left down a side street and watched the red car drive past without slowing down. Steve breathed a sigh of relief and kept driving, making a few more turns down side streets to get him back to the main road.

Ten minutes later he pulled into the parking lot of his building and parked. He got out and began walking towards the building on the far side of the lot. The rain had almost let up by now, but Steve didn't care. He was already soaked to the bone. He had dried a little bit on the ride home, but was still uncomfortably wet.

As he walked, he noticed something out of the corner of his eye. Amidst all the grey, white, and black cars, he saw a red one. A Dodge. "Fuck off," he told himself as he slowed his steps. He squinted to look at the licence plate. He couldn't remember if it was the same as the one from before.

"Snap out of it, Steve, you're seeing ghosts," he said to himself out loud. He picked up his pace, but heard wet footsteps behind him. He turned his neck casually but saw nothing. "Fuck sakes," he muttered to himself, "now you really are seeing ghosts, and talking to yourself."

Steve knew the mental game. It happened when you were stressed and paranoid. You begin thinking that people were after you. That everyone you saw was an enemy. You heard footfalls and saw shadows. Heard noises that never happened. Even though he knew all this, and that what he saw and heard now was probably just in his head, he couldn't shake the feeling that he was being followed.

He made it to the building, went inside, and up to his apartment. He closed the door and locked it, breathing a sigh of relief when he felt the lock clunk into place. Steve walked over to his fridge and got a beer. He popped it open and took a long swig from the bottle. He swallowed and exhaled with an, "Ahhhhh."

Steve plopped down into his chair and began to think about everything. "Okay, who would do this?" he asked himself. He looked at the obvious fact that was screaming at him. It happened in movies all the time. Why not here? Team betrayal. Selfishness. One member of the group wanted it all for himself. Steve knew he hadn't killed anyone. Frank. He was so cool and calm at the two apartments, like he'd seen it all before, but it was too obvious. It couldn't be him, could it? Steve thought back over the last few days, since the night of the heist. He and Kev had gone off alone at that one point, but Kev just wanted a cigarette, and Frank was making a call to Tony. That did take a little longer than Steve expected. Maybe that was when they made some deal? Yes, that could work. Steve sat up in his chair.

"Okay," he said out loud to the empty room. "Kev and Frank talk, and make some deal where they get to keep the money for themselves. They decide to kill Jack, and then me? But they didn't come after me. Wouldn't I have been next? Fuck. That doesn't make sense. Why would he kill Kev? Unless..." He took another swig of beer. "Unless

Frank wanted to kill Kev after me, but Kev might get the same greedy idea to kill him and might see it coming, so Frank decides to kill Kev before me. Kev wouldn't see it coming." Steve finished his beer, went back to the fridge and grabbed another.

"And, Frank keeps telling us to go home and stay there until we hear from him. He knows where we'll be the whole time. He can just show up for some reason and kill each of us. Fuck, man that's gotta be it! No way that shit is gonna work on me! I'll be ready for him." Steve got up and went to his bedroom, got the box from under his bed, and pulled out his gun. He screwed on the silencer and put the gun under his pillow. "Just like Bond," he said to himself. He drank the rest of the beer, threw on an old pair of shorts, and climbed into bed. He lay there for the next few hours, clutching the gun, pointing it at the ceiling and other random things around his room, practicing for when his killer would arrive.

Steve woke up to the sound of his phone going off. He rolled over and looked at it. Two new texts. He opened the messages, both from Frank. One was an hour old. It read *Meet at the parking garage from the other night, one hour* The next message read *Sorry, got tied up with the kids. Be there soon* Steve looked at the times of the messages again. He had slept right through the first one. "Ah, shit," he said, looking at the time on his phone. 12:33 p.m.

"Well, I guess I should head there now," he said to himself, followed by, "I need to stop talking to myself."

Steve was sitting on the edge of his bed when he heard something at his door. He got up quietly and peered out of his bedroom at the front door to his apartment. He heard the clicking of lock picks. "Oh shit," he said. He scrambled back into his room and reached under his pillow for his gun, but found nothing. "Fuck!" he whispered. "Where did I put it?" He looked around his room. He scanned his room again until his eyes fell on it, lying on a pile of laundry. He went to reach for it when he froze. The sound of his front door opening glued his feet to the floor. He had two options. Go for the gun and give away his position, or slide under the bed and hide. He elected for option two, and slid down to his knees and crawled under the bed. His bed was in the corner of the room. He reached up and pulled the covers over the side to help hide the gap under the bed, and hope-fully hide any clue he was under there. He belly-crawled along the floor until he was face down and up against the walls, as far as possible from the open side of the bed.

He heard heavy footsteps walking through his apartment. He heard cupboards open and close, cushions turned over and put back. Whoever was out there was looking for some-thing.

The footsteps got closer to his bedroom. The knob turned, and the door slowly opened. Steve felt his heart in his throat and heard it beating like thunderclaps. He covered his mouth to try to muffle his breathing. The blood was rushing through him, and he could hear it in his ears. Adren-aline began surging through his system as the intruder en-tered the bedroom. Steve looked out from under the bed and saw his gun, still on the pile of laundry. If he inched forward, he might be able to reach it. He could see the feet aimed at his closet and heard the intruder pushing aside the clothes and boxes inside.

Steve inched forward, leaning out towards the gun,

stretching his arm as far as it could go. He reached and grazed the edge of the laundry before he snapped his arm back at the sound of the feet moving. He looked out from under the bed, looked at the floor, and saw the intruder on one knee, opening boxes. *What is he looking for?* Steve thought to himself.

Steve turned back to the pile of laundry and the gun. He slid another few inches across the floor, careful not to make any noise. He looked back at the intruder, still on one knee facing away from the bed. Steve reached out, his fingers now grazing the handle of the gun. Then he got an idea. He grabbed the edge of the pile of laundry and began to slide it towards him, ever so slowly. The gun jostled on top and tilted towards the floor. Steve held his breath and stopped pulling as the gun teetered, millimetres from the floor. He looked back at the intruder and saw boxes being pushed back into the closet. Steve reached forward with both hands now, one pulling the clothes pile and the other reaching for the gun to grab it once it was in reach. He gave one last tug as he saw the intruder rise from his knee. The pile slid back to Steve, the gun tilted and fell, the end of the silencer bouncing off his index finger. Steve grabbed the gun with both hands and pulled it back towards his body. He turned it in his hand, slid back, and pressed his body up against the wall again. He pointed the gun out at the room in the direction of the intruder, who began to walk across the room, towards the bed. The toes pointed directly at Steve's face. He steadied the gun with both hands, sliding his thumb over the safety and flicking it off. He placed his finger over the trigger, hovering there, waiting for the slightest indication that the intruder had detected him. He would fire one shot into his leg, and when the intruder fell, he would empty the clip into the rest of the body. Steve's hands were shaking slightly. The adrenaline surged through his body. His heart beat faster as he readied his mind to pull that trigger when a phone went off. The ring was familiar. He had heard it before, but he was so focussed he couldn't quite place it, until he heard the intruder's voice answer the call.

"Yeah? Now? Okay. I'll be there," he said into the phone. "Fuckin' kids ruin everything," he said out loud.

Frank.

Steve had known it would be him. He wasn't sure, but now he knew it was all true. Everything he thought of last night made sense and was confirmed now. He heard Frank walk out of the bedroom and leave the apartment. Steve let out the breath he had been holding the last two minutes.

"Holy Fuck!" he cried out. "I knew it, I knew it, I fucking knew it!" Steve said to himself as he paced his bedroom. He looked at the gun in his hand and flipped the safety back on. He sat on the edge of his bed. He couldn't believe this was how it was going to go down. After all the shit they had been through over the years. All the previous jobs, legal and illegal. The good times at the bar, the stories they all shared. It all meant nothing now. All those memories meant nothing when large amounts of money were involved.

Steve's phone went off again. Another new text message had arrived. Again, it was from Frank. *Apparently, Tony was wrong. The first message he got was that the guy had left, not that he was here. Sorry to make you go out for nothing* it read.

"What the fuck?" Steve said to himself. "That lying fucker. But, okay. He wanted me out of my place. Why?

Didn't he want to kill me? Unless he wanted to wait in here for when I got back and then bam! Fuckin' hell. What luck that his kids did cause a problem. Fuck, he would've been here!" Steve was smiling at his luck. "Well, now it's my turn. I'm going to get that son of a bitch, in his house."

Steve decided to wait until tomorrow before going to confront Frank. "I'll get the answers and the book from him. He wants to take me out and keep it for himself? I don't think so."

Nineteen

Steve had been to Frank's house a few times, and he re-membered the address. He sat in his car, parked across the street from Frank's driveway. The sky had cleared overnight. The sun shone down from the blue sky above, drying up the ground. The heat was back, along with the humidity, and Steve was beginning to sweat as the remaining cool air from the ride over dissipated.

Steve had spent the night thinking about how today would go. What he would say to Frank. He imagined Frank's look of surprise when he walked in on him, explaining that he had figured it out and knew everything. He smiled at the thought of fear and panic on Frank's face, feeling righteous as he avenged the death of his two friends. Steve had never condoned killing on their previous jobs, but now, he was all for it. Nothing would stop him. It felt right. He knew it was right. He had to stop Frank.

Steve had been sitting in his car for fifteen minutes now. The only car in the driveway was Frank's. His wife was gone and so were the kids. Frank was all alone. Time to say hello.

Steve tucked his gun into the back of his pants and pulled his damp shirt over the handle, hiding it from view. He walked to the driveway from his car and up to the front door. He rang the doorbell. No answer. Steve stepped back and looked at the house. All was still. He looked back to make sure he hadn't hallucinated Frank's van in the driveway. It was there. He rang the doorbell again. Nothing. Confusion fell over Steve like a shadow. He wiped the sweat from his brow and banged on the door with his fist thinking that maybe the doorbell was broken. He waited a few minutes and then banged again. He stepped back from the door and off the front porch onto the path. He looked over the house again, then down the street. There were a few cars parked in driveways and a couple more farther down the street. Steve chuckled to himself as he saw a red car ten houses down, parked on the street. "Seeing those ghosts again," he said to himself.

He turned back to the front door, his knock still unanswered. Steve began to wonder if Frank had come to the door or looked through a window and seen him, figured out why he was here, and was either hiding or getting ready for him inside. Either way, Steve didn't want to wait any longer. He reached out and tried the door. Unlocked.

Steve stepped in through the front door and closed it behind him quietly with one hand, pulling out his gun with his other hand. He stepped softly down the hallway, gun pointed up and ready, his finger hovering over the trigger. The adrenaline was back from last night, coursing through him. His heartbeat quickened, and he felt his hands shake ever so slightly. He looked into the living room as he passed it. It was empty. He walked into the kitchen.

In the middle of the kitchen was the counter and behind the counter, on the floor, was blood. It was flowing, slowly, but still flowing. It was fresh. Steve lowered his gun as he leaned forward and squinted, looking at the pool of blood on the white tile floor. He walked forward and peered around to the corner to see Frank's lifeless body with red fluid seeping from underneath. One gunshot to the head. He stepped back, and as he did, he felt the cold steel of a gun barrel press against the back of his neck. He froze.

The combination of cold steel and fright sent shivers up his back, and the hairs on his neck and arms stood on end. His mouth fell open, and his eyes grew wide.

A gloved hand reached around and took his gun from his hand. Steve turned slowly to face the assassin. The gun lifted off his neck allowing him to turn.

Steve's heart was beating faster than he could ever have imagined possible. Sweat beaded on his forehead and trickled down his spine. His mouth was wide open and dry. He knew he had reached the end. He knew his death was coming. There was no way out. His three friends were dead. He was next. He didn't understand anything anymore. He had been so sure it was Frank behind everything, but he was dead, and there was still someone pointing a gun at him. Steve raised his head to see the stranger, dressed all in black with a ski mask pulled over his head. Steve could see a smile through the mouth slit. He could see the look of joy in the eyes that looked back at him.

"Oh, this is rich," said the stranger. "You know, I didn't peg you for the smartest one of the group, but the other three, well they're dead first, aren't they?"

"Who the fuck are you?" Steve spat out.

"It has been a fun couple of days, hasn't it? So much has happened. All so quickly, too! And smoothly! I knew you guys could do it."

"Who the fuck are you?!" Steve spat out again. "How

do you know us? Why are you doing this?"

"The same reason as you, my friend. For this." He held up a duffle bag and threw it at Steve's feet. Steve recognized it. The zipper was half open, and he could see the folio inside.

"You know about that? How the fuck do you know about that?" Steve yelled as he tried to look through the mask. Steve looked down at the bag that was just thrown at his feet. A thought flashed through his mind. *Tony? Did he betray us?* Steve looked up at the person in front of him. He looked at the skin through the eye and mouth holes in the mask. *White guy, so nope, not Tony. Who is this?*

"Of course I know about this ol' thing," the stranger said, smirking behind his mask. "It was my idea, wasn't it?" He reached up and pulled the mask of his face.

"Fuck. No way. Fuck off. It can't be..." Steve's voice trailed off.

"Yep," said Matthew.

"What in the fuck is going on?" Steve said with desperation. "You're in fuckin' high school! How the fuck did you do all this?!"

"Enough with your cursing, Steve. It's quite unnecessary. I'll do you the favour I did the rest of your friends. I'll ease the pain of confusion, and then I'll ease the pain of life," he said smiling.

Steve looked at Matthew in shock. He had completely forgotten about him. He was the originator of the idea. The first person to mention the folio. Sure, they lost the construction job and had no use for him, so he disappeared, but now that he thought about it, Matthew never called again in the days that followed to find out about any new work. He had completely fallen out of Steve's mind.

He looked at the kid in front of him. No more than eighteen, and yet he had somehow masterminded this. "You, you planned this? Bullshit."

"Is it so hard to believe? Well, maybe for the simple minds of your little group," said Matthew mockingly.

"Fuck you."

"Yes. Fuck me. Sorry, Steve. You thought you were so smart, didn't you? Put it all together. Thought you had it down. So did Frank. He thought you were behind it all. Even went to your place to see if there was any evidence he could find. He probably would have killed you too, but, alas, family life intervened."

"How the hell do you know this?"

"Please," Matthew said. Steve thought about it. *Guess he was following everyone.*

"There you go," said Matthew. "Putting it together in your head now. Yes, there it is," he said as he saw the confusion on Steve's face replaced with understanding. "You were being followed, but you gave up on that too easily, because you thought it was Frank. You almost had me last night in that parking lot outside your building."

Steve was putting together his thoughts but was still missing parts. "So, you planned this from the start? How did you know we would do it? How did you know about our other jobs? Did you even know about them?"

"Of course," said Matthew matter-of-factly. "You know, Jack is that dumb. He would occasionally let things slip while at work. I put it together. You pull little jobs. One night I followed you to that jewellery store. You pulled it off quite nicely. I figured you had the potential for a greater score. You just needed the right push. I couldn't steal the folio myself, I don't quite have the means, but you did. I introduced the thought and then helped give you that push. Losing your job and having expenses does lead some people to make bold decisions," Matthew said smiling.

"You got us fired?"

"Sort of. I suggested it. Helped the boss make the right decision. Told him I knew of a better, cheaper crew he could replace you guys with."

"How did you do all this? You're a fucking kid!"

Matthew smiled, turning his gun over in his hand.

The gun was the same as Steve's. The same as Kev's, Frank's, Jack's too. Matthew noticed Steve staring at the gun. "Recognize this?" He said pointing the gun at Steve. "It's Jack's. I wasn't going to kill any of you with *my* gun. Hah! That would be stupid. No, I took Jack's when I broke into his place to kill him. He didn't hide it very well. Bedside table drawer. Too easy, but like I said, he's not that smart.

"The police may never realize that the folio is missing, you took care of that part with the fire, but when your bodies are found, it's going to look like you murdered everyone. Started with Jack, killing him with his gun and then Kev, who was on to you, then Frank who was too threatening to let live, and finally, you took your own life, unable to live with the guilt. Open and shut."

"How is that open and shut?"

"Because it's an answer, and that's all the police want. It wraps everything up neatly." Steve knew he was right. If an answer presented itself to the police, they would take it without looking twice.

"And now, I must leave you, or rather, you must leave

me, and this world." Matthew raised the gun to Steve's head. He picked up the folio in the bag at Steve's feet and took a few steps back. "Thanks again," he said as he shook the duffle bag.

Steve felt his heart race. *I can't let this little shit win. We worked too hard for this score, and he's just gonna walk away with it all? Pin it all on me?! No! I won't let my friends die like that. I won't die like that.*

Steve lunged forward at Matthew who half-expected it and fired a shot at Steve. The bullet grazed his shoulder as Steve crashed into Matthew, tackling him to the floor. The gun fired off a second shot as Matthew's arm smacked into the floor, the bullet tearing through the drywall on his left.

Steve rolled off of Matthew, grabbing at his wounded shoulder. He cupped his hand over his wound and looked at his hand, seeing blood. He turned his head to try to see the wound and saw the hole in his shirt growing redder.

Matthew was scrambling to his knees beside Steve, spinning around to aim the gun, but Steve saw him turning, lashed out with his right leg, kicking the gun from his hand, another shot firing off into the ceiling.

Matthew grunted and got up onto his feet, backing away from Steve as he got up too.

"You can't get away with this. I won't let you," said Steve.

"Please, you can't handle me. I will destroy you!" Matthew yelled lunging forward and grabbing Steve's arms.

Matthew used his momentum to drive Steve backwards, slamming him into the counter. Steve arched back over the counter, and as his head turned to the side, he saw the knife block. Steve brought his knee up into Matthew's groin.

Matthew eased up slightly in recoil, putting more room between the two men, and Steve brought his knee up again into Matthew's midsection.

Matthew crumpled to the ground in a heap, groaning and clutching his stomach. Steve staggered back and over to the knife block, pulling out the large chef's knife from the top slot. He took a fighting stance over Matthew who looked up and saw the knife. He spun on the ground and used his legs to push himself off the counter, sliding across the floor around the corner of the kitchen island. He rolled over and scrambled to his feet with Steve following behind him with the knife in his hand.

Steve charged at Matthew, slashing at the air with the blade. Matthew dodged each swipe in turn, ducking and dodging left, right, up and down. He jumped back at a stabbing thrust, the blade nicking his shirt. Rage took Steve over as he pushed forward, knife held out like a bayonette. Matthew backed up, stumbling and knocking over a chair at the kitchen table, and then smacked into the wall. Steve rushed toward Matthew and screamed as he reached forward. Matthew grabbed his free hand by the wrist and tried to angle himself away from the knife hand. He leaned back and twisted, avoiding the thrust from Steve, then, grabbing the knife hand, leaned forward and head-butted Steve in the forehead.

Steve staggered back, dropping the knife. His world went black for half a second. He reached up to his head with both hands and felt the warm, wet blood trickling out of the wound where Matthew's skull had connected with his. He let out an enraged, pain-filled roar. Matthew flung himself past Steve, diving toward his gun. Steve wiped the blood from his forehead and turned to see Matthew crawling towards the gun. He gritted his teeth as he jumped on top of him, stopping Matthew a few feet short of the gun.

Steve grabbed the back of Matthew's head by his hair and pulled it up, slamming him face down down into the tile floor. Matthew thrashed underneath, trying to roll over and push Steve off. Steve slammed Matthew's head into the floor two more times before Matthew was able to half roll underneath his attacker, and kick up with his legs, pushing Steve off.

Matthew grabbed his face as he got to his knees, screaming in pain. His nose was broken and blood streamed out of it, down his face dripping on the floor. "You fucker!"

Steve managed half a smirk as he got up on his feet. He hunched over, tired, but ready for more. Matthew ran at him and bear hugged him. Steve threw punches into Matthew's kidneys, each landing with heavy groans from both men. Matthew pushed off and wound up his punch, but Steve blocked and parried with his uppercut to the gut. Matthew let out a whoosh of air with a stifled grunt and came back at Steve with a left jab. Landing the jab, Matthew followed it up with a right hook and a left uppercut, both connecting to Steve's chin. The combo sent Steve reeling backward, leaning up against the wall, his face aimed at the floor. He saw the knife.

Steve crouched down, lightning quick, and retrieved the knife. Looking up, he saw Matthew wiping the blood from his nose and the tears from his eyes. He was standing beside the gun. It rested on the ground by his right foot. He was about eleven feet from Steve, who looked at the knife in his hand, then down at the gun on the floor, that Matthew had now spotted, and then up at Matthew's face.

Steve had heard of the twenty-one-foot rule, and since he only had eleven feet to cover, knew he could close the gap in half the one point five seconds, meaning Matthew had to pick up and draw the gun in half a second. *He can't,* Steve thought to himself, a wry smile peeking across his lips.

The two men made eye contact, and each knew what the other was thinking. Matthew took a step to the side, putting the gun right between his legs. The two men stood in a showdown for what felt like minutes. As soon as he saw the slightest movement in Steve's body, Matthew closed his feet, trapping the gun, reached behind him onto the counter, throwing the newspaper that lay there. The pages scattered into the air and slowed Steve for the instant Matthew needed. He flicked his feet and flipped the gun into the air in a soccer-style move, catching the gun, and pulling the trigger just as Steve crashed into him.

The gun fired, and the two men crashed into the floor, Steve falling on top of Matthew. Matthew pushed and rolled Steve off and onto the floor. He looked and saw the gunshot he made, right in Steve's head. Blood streamed out of the hole.

Matthew smiled, he had won. He moved to get up, but felt a tremendous pain in his stomach as he moved. He looked down and saw only the hilt of the chef's knife Steve had held. He felt his back dampen as the blood trickled out. He tried to pull the knife, but the pain was overwhelming. More blood began to ooze out of the wound as he moved the knife. He let go and let his arms fall to his side. He looked straight up as his eyelids closed and the world faded to black.

Epilogue

Detective Marcus Cole groaned as he got out of his car. He parked a few feet outside the caution tape that had been put up by the uniformed officers when they first arrived on the scene a few hours earlier. Cole grabbed his coffee, closed his door, and walked towards the nearest officer. He flashed his badge and nodded at the officer who was lifting the tape allowing him to duck under into the crime scene.

Cole was tired from the long day. He had run out of leads for the two murders that had fallen onto his desk on successive days. Two men shot dead, each in his own apartment. One in the bedroom, one in the bathroom. Both crime scenes had been wiped clean of any evidence. The only thing the coroner had been able to tell him was that the gunshots were identical, made by the same calibre bullet from the same gun.

He knew the two murders were connected, but in the first twenty-four hours, he had found nothing substantial to connect the two other than who they were, and that they worked together. The apartments had been registered to a Kevin Martin and Jack Stanley; both were employed with "MackoCon," a small construction company.

Cole walked up the front path passing more uniformed officers standing watch or talking to neighbours and the crime scene unit members in their lab coats carrying cameras and samples to and from the house. He walked past an officer who was questioning a middle-aged woman, with two little girls huddled around her legs, sobbing. The officer was trying his best to comfort her and get answers to his questions. He stepped inside the door, and found his partner, Gerrard Hadfield, standing in the kitchen.

"Hey, Gerry," said Cole as he walked in, sipping his coffee. "What do we got?"

"Look around, man," said Gerry. "Three bodies, two shot, one stabbed...and guess what," he said pointing at the largest corpse, "the same bullet wound as the other two vics."

"Get out!" Cole said. "Great. What about these two?" He pointed at the stabbing victim and the second gunshot victim. As he panned over the room, he spotted the knife and gun on the floor, each with yellow evidence number cards beside it.

"That guy, gunshot, same as the two I just mentioned, and that," he said pointing, "is most likely the gun. Need ballistics to confirm, but the first speculation is that's it."

"Okay, so stabbed guy is the shooter, the gun is next to him, and he wasn't shot."

"Best case, yeah."

"And then the stabber is him?" Cole asked pointing.

"Yep. Gotta check fingerprints on the knife there, but seems like it, yeah."

Cole looked over the room and the signs of the fight that had taken place. He surveyed the evidence lying before him. "Did you come to a conclusion?" he asked his partner.

"Yeah, but let's see what you got," said Gerry with a smile.

"One question first," Cole said. "Whose house?"

"Big guy's. Wife called it in when she got home with the two kids after school."

"And let me guess, we have an ID, and he works with those other two from yesterday and earlier this morning."

"Yeah. And?"

"And," Cole said, dragging out the word as he thought, "with this guy too," he said pointing at Steve's body.

"Yep. Big guy is Frank Mackolo, his wife Jessica and two daughters are outside," Gerry explained. "And he is Steven Miller."

"And this fifth wheel?"

"No idea. Not yet. No I.D. on him. Gotta wait till we run prints and dental. So now you know pretty much what I know, and have asked more than your 'one question,' what happened?"

"Frank was at home when the mystery man walks in. There was no struggle, so either he caught him by surprise, or he knew him—look into that, maybe he worked with them too—there was some dispute among the group, Frank, Steve, and those other two, Kevin and Jack. Something went bad leading to this mystery man killing each of them one at a time—so again, I think they worked together in some way. Steve, there, was dropping by Frank, maybe to settle things or discuss the fact that two of their friends were dead, or missing if they didn't know already. Or maybe they were in it together and were going to escape together, but he walked in on, or just after, the shooting. Steve and Mystery Man struggle, fight, and end with stabbing and gunshot," finished Cole.

"I came to the same ending. Something got these guys

all in a tizzy, but that part, I don't know."

"Had to be money."

"Financials of the first two were barren, not much in the accounts. Just enough to last out the last week or two of the month. Waiting on results from these two, got someone checking it out n—" Gerry was cut off by his phone ringing. "Speak of the devil. Hadfield here. Yeah. And the other one? Really? Okay, thanks." Gerry had a puzzled look on his face.

"What'd they say?"

"Financials are clean. No huge amounts in, no huge amounts missing. No big money problems either way."

"So, maybe this fifth guy had the money?"

"Maybe it wasn't money?"

"Well, what then?"

"We searched the house?"

"Most of it, nothing yet. I'll get CSU to do a more thorough sweep, look for possible hiding spots or secret drawers and such. Maybe there's something somewhere."

"There has to be. This isn't random. We should go back and check the other apartments too. Find out where this Steve lived, check his place, and find out who the hell the fifth man is," Cole said, walking out of the house with Gerry following close behind.

They stopped in the driveway, Gerry looking over the notes he had just made and Cole looking out at the houses and down the street. He sighed and began to walk back to his car.

Several houses away from the police yellow tape sat a black Cadillac Escalade. Past the tinted windows, inside the vehicle, sat a well dressed man. Black suit, black tie, black

Ray-Ban sunglasses. He sat quietly watching the people gathering outside along the police barrier, watching to see what was going on, and what had happened inside the house. He felt his phone vibrate with an incoming call and swiped right to answer. "Police are here. No. Yes, I have it," he said, patting the dufflebag in passenger seat. The call ended, he started up the Escalade and drove down the street, away from the crowd of people and sirens flashing.

Chris Eyles lives in Mississauga, Ontario where he spends most of his time playing video games, writing, watching movies and playing hockey. He studied Professional Writing at York University and graduated with a Bachelor of Arts with Honors. This is his first novel. In his spare time he also cosplays and makes costumes.

Twitter.com/ChrisEyles
Instagram.com/ChrisEyles

CPSIA information can be obtained
at www.ICGtesting.com
Printed in the USA
BVHW042035010521
606175BV00006B/62